Protecting

Beauty

Thomas Tyme

Library of Congress Control Number: 2013941589
San # 920-5861 Fleming Tyme Publishing
Copyright © 2015- 3rd edition, revised. Vol. I.

Printed in the USA.
ISBN-13: 9780989521819
ISBN-10: 0989521818

For information address: Fleming Tyme Publishing
tflemingtyme@gmail.com

FTyP

An imprint of Fleming Tyme Publishing

ACKNOWLEDGMENTS

I thank Judy for allowing precious time alone to write and for proof readings. Additional thanks goes to Karin Szwec for lending her professional suggestions and Jim Fleming for reminding me to write for the readers.

PROLOGUE

This is a story of a beautiful place where fresh air and bountiful resources excite the senses. Friendly animals, gorgeous waters, lush farmlands and majestic mountains are an everyday cause for song in the Beaulancians hearts. However, an unaware reckoning with evil is on the way against their nirvana lifestyle. It happens in the midst of our own Earthly existence. Fearful people scramble for their lives in another realm, dimension, zone, or call it what you will. Their location is out of our reach. An evil terrorist determines to inflict death upon everything and everyone. The inhabitants' known as Beaulancians have bravely and successfully fought against wicked overthrowing dictators in the past. Their victories have always been aided from above. Beaulancia is a sacred place.

This invasion is unlike any ever before. To lose this fight would mean the end of Beautyland. Not to win means death to all, not just some. Going on the defense is not a question but how? This is a story of battling pure evil. Beaulancians know it comes down to the success of man's alignment to the horses sent by the most demonstrative God to protect and defend Beautyland. There may come a day when we see horses coming through the sky but as of now they have arrived in Beautyland. This bountiful and kind place will find these four horses strong and magically pulling their loads of deadly struggles gladly. As it goes; Bandy, the beautiful mare leads the studs; Utopio, Spirit and Astro in Protecting Beauty.

BEAUTY LAND

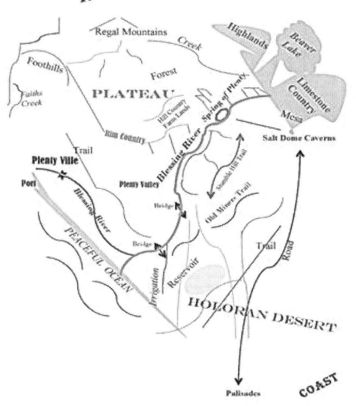

Chapter 1

THE DISCOVERY

❦

Today is not the first time angelic equines from Folkhaven came to intercede for Beautyland. There were many days spent in the long ago battling Blaze Evil. The last time we all wanted to render him lifeless. Instead, the supreme deities spared our might and let him exist. Now he returns from exile to destroy all of Beautyland. We must obliterate him for good. One does not escape inner fire. The center shrinks and the outer edges grow. Very proper agents must extinguish this menace once and for always. Three of my most courageous and adventurous studs have arrived. They will learn about themselves and grow in the time of their lives.

In this distant dimensional sphere of which no one knows, there does exist a people facing more difficult realities of envy, hate and reckonings than anyone has ever witnessed. The Spring of Plenty nourishes the region and enters into the Blessing River providing abundance for Beaulancians. It allows for a green valley, fishing, frolicking through fauna, flourishing flora, creatures and humans alike!

I will take you through what trials await by describing in detail the misadventures facing Beaulancians and the defenses put up. My name is Bandy. These other three, best of the best, warrior horses have no idea what they are in for but will soon find out. This is in real time. Actions occur during the living story.

Clickidy, click, ditterrump, ditterrump, clickidy, click, ditterrump, ditter-rump, clickidy, click.

"Oh, the grass is green and gold, green and gold, green and gold. I am so hungry this morning. Yum-mity-yum, yum-mity-yum, I love to eat in the morning!"

Astro runs through the grassland, frolicking through the gorgeous fields of Beautyland. He sounds off his pleasure in song.

"Oh, how many blades can I eat in a day? More than I could of regular hay, ha-ha, ti-da, ti-da, ti-da!"

His cousin shouts, "Whenie-aw-ewe-henie-haw!"

Spirit the more intelligent brother of Astro, asks, "Utopio, what noise you make? Is it a disorderly butterfly or what?"

The strongest and fastest stallion finds trouble when about to drink from what only yesterday was a clear freshwater river that tasted like honeysuckle. Eerily, a scent so vile now causes his head to shake.

He says, "Woo-wee smell this."

"Smell what?" begs Spirit.

"I thought I smelled something funny too," says Astro.

"Take a good whiff. Tell me what it is," requests Utopio.

"Well, I would say yuck! Yep, that is what I smell. I smell stinky yuk in the water," Astro responds.

Spirit replies, "The water is so cloudy it is polluted. Do not drink. We have to find out what is happening here! Something is wrong. Let's go upstream."

Utopio agrees, "You're right! Let's get to it and try to make some sense of this!"

Spirit suggests, "We should look at the mound where the Spring of Plenty flows into the river from the red cliff."

"Yeah, let's trot over there and check it out," Astro agrees.

Utopio states, "If we keep a good pace, we can make it there by nightfall."

Traveling in single file, the three horses move over rocky ground. Wild mustangs grazing in lower meadows seem unaware of any unnatural occurrence.

The bountiful land never ceases to amaze Astro. Pecan and apple orchards fill his eyes with delight. He trips on a root and stumbles down the hill. He stops in front of an apple tree and drools.

Utopio shouts, "Are you all right?"

"I sure am. This trip led to apples. Ha-ha, I am going to eat a few."

Spirit remarks, "Well, do not fall far behind."

"The day is getting warm. Our tongues are drying out. We could all use some apples. We have not had any water since sunup," says Utopio.

"Come on, I'll save the big ones for you," Astro replies.

Spirit describes, "What a sight—coexisting trees, Apple, Peach, Cherry, Pecans, Sequoias, Redwoods, Pines, Spruce, Oaks, Ash, Willows, Cottonwoods, Walnut, Birch, Maple, Dogwood, Beech, Elm, and Aspen. Here we have shade, food, water and red rock views. Is this not the most beautiful place you have ever seen?"

"It is my grateful cousin but we cannot drink the water. Eat up and we will inspect it once more before leaving," Utopio instructs.

"It stinks," says Astro.

"OK! Take what you want with you. We are going." Utopio replies.

Astro acknowledges, "I feel great after that." Spirit Suggests, "Once we get up this rise the rest of the way looks easy."

Utopio suddenly rears, warning, "Whoa, watch out, it's a venomous snake, stay back!"

It heaves its body into an "s" and rattles its tail all the while hissing. It is about to strike when squelched by the powerful hoof of Utopio. He rears in a Stallion like pose and mightily comes down on it breaking it's back it in a fit of fury.

"You got him! The diamond back never had a chance," shouts Astro

"You flattened its head in the nick of time," says Spirit.

Astro replies, "Yep, I wonder what would have happened if it bit you.

"All right, let's get out of here. Keep your eyes peeled for wolves and cougars," Utopio warns.

"I am not afraid, "Get along little horse's, get along we go. Following our leader Utopio over any trail, we are unafraid to go. We go, we go, we go, we go," sings Astro.

Ten minutes later, he asks, "How much farther is it?"

Spirit says, "In another fifteen minutes, we should see a mound on the other side of the river. The spring is there and we have to crossover to get to it."

"I hope there is not any smelly mischief where we cross. I usually get water in my mouth when I swim," Astro replies.

"I do too and I sure am thirsty. I could really use a drink," says Spirit.

Utopio spots a bald eagle on the edge of a cliff and point's his nose saying, "Look up there!"

"It's Scout. Can you see the river, Scout? Astro asks.

The eagle who can only speak in rhymes swoops down onto a boulder next to Utopio, saying, "Hello, majestic steeds you are a beautiful sight. Are deeds you here to do with might? The lowland is where to graze and you are off by a long ways. You are lathered wet, where are you trying to get?"

Spirit asks, "How far is the river from here, Scout?"

He says, "Well, if you go by hoof, not in air over roof, maybe one hour not too sour. Take steep slope on left, do not stumble, break neck, jump big crevice, and make time less. If you squeeze through the breezeway between the bluffs and climb over the rocky precipice, you can cut around. . ."

"Wait, wait, wait, Scout! Stop, that is good enough," Spirit, resounds.

Scout asks, "Why the river you going?"

"We're going for a showing," Astro answers.

Scout asks, "Knowing showing or showing knowing?"

"It's the scenic way from Apple Valley," Spirit replies.

"Why hurry, scurry, Studley-Dudley?"

"OK, OK, we don't know for sure. We are trying to find the source of a repulsive smell in the river. The southern stream is putrid," Utopio exclaims!

"It is not natural. Something is wrong! Yesterday, we drank cool sweet water," Spirit adds.

"It was pure and quenching but not anymore," Utopio explains.

"Hope no dopes spoil with soaps. Flow will show and you will know. Churning, turning, burning, I get it but cannot let it. We want no mucko to make water uckoh," Scout assures.

Spirit suggests, "We sense a dark force at the spring."

"Screech, you suspect a prank, at the bank. Scout search for you hosses and make privy any losses.

"We will inspect the river at the spring," Utopio replies.

"I will follow the flow beyond the ridge and roam. If mine eyes do conundrums solve, for any dooms on the scene, to you alone I will show and tell, of what spoils to clean, screech!"

"Thanks, Scout," they exclaim as he flies away.

Astro sings another ditty, "We have Scout looking out, at what is all about? He will tell us through the breeze what lies beyond the trees. Scout is in route, look out, look out!"

Spirit completes the didy with "He no doubt will find out!"

"OK, brothers, keep quiet and stay focused," says Utopio.

"Right, we do not want to get lost," Spirit agrees.

Astro says, "Message received and noted. Not another word, I am focused."

"Studs, gather around here and look at this."

Spirit asks, "What is it, Topio old boy?"

"Horse tracks pull wagons toward the creek. Why would the Beaulancians take wagons over a narrow elk trail?"

Spirit further asks, "Astro, what are you looking at?"

"I see seven or eight dog tracks outside the wheel marks."

"How fresh are they," asks Utopio?

"Well, they might be a day old," says Spirit.

With a fierce determination in his voice, Utopio adds, "Let's keep going. We should find out more as we follow. They lead toward the river. Move on mighty ones and keep an eye out!"

He bolts away with a cringing intuition about the wagons and mentally readies himself for battle. A cornered horse comes out fighting or escapes by running over its adversaries. This most powerful horse is preparing for the worst. They are not ordinary and display celestially different traits. They can handle themselves in a skirmish with formidable abilities. The river valley now appears in plain view and Utopio remarks, "There's the spring!"

Astro notices an opportunity with wide-open eyes saying,

"Let's dine on the grass next to the river and try the water before we swim across. I am thirsty and famished. How about it guys?"

"I could use some sustenance before crossing," Spirit agrees.

Utopio replies, "No overeating boys remember we have work to do, before nightfall!"

"The other side near the spring looks cloudy. I am going to nibble my way upriver and try a drink," says Astro.

Spirit and Utopio chow down on climax grass as Astro sips, gulps, and vacuums drinks up his long throat. He shouts, "The water is good up here fellas!"

"Astro, we're right next to you," Spirit replies.

"Oh!"

Topio drinks, lifts his head, shakes and whinnies saying,

"Ha, that's the stuff. Great gulps of natural joy."

"Make room for me," Spirit replies and squeezes between the two.

Astro edges his way downstream to appraise wagon tracks going across. A muddy trail exits on the other side, he shouts, "They crossed here!"

"Let's go," snorts Spirit.

Utopio trots across the river over a narrow slippery slab of solid rock.

"Come on, I see imprints leading to the mound entrance," he says.

Spirit whispers, "It is a cavern above the spring. Yellow water is pouring out below. Someone is really polluting the river."

"A hunch is a hunch, of course, of course, until followed by a reasonable horse," Astro answers.

"And my nose, knows, whoever made these tracks did it," replies Utopio.

"Right, let's sneak up this slope and get a better look from the ridge," says Spirit.

"Good idea brother we will just blend in unnoticed,".

A vicious jackal dog lunges at Utopio from behind a Juniper tree. It latches onto his throat. He twists, turns, and bites at the hanging beast but to no avail. He starts to perform a special defense when suddenly a wild mountain lion jumps onto the jackal's back. It fiercely claws its head, gouging out its eyes and it falls off. Utopio quickly kicks it in the chest sending it hard against a jagged cliff. A sharp wet rock sliver pierces through the blaggard's heart and holds him there.

"Way to go. Who was that lion," asks Astro?

Utopio answers, "Watch your backs. He is still loose."

Scout circles in the sky above screeching, "Do not worry about the lion. He is a friend of mine."

"Where have you been did you see the fight," asks Astro?

"I came, I saw and I caused the claws."

Spirit asks, "What do you mean?"

He explains, "I flew over the clover and saw the waiting rover. I recruited the puma, Sabertoes, to end its muted blows. He has watched the mound since yesterday and saw strangers hide away. Doggies guarded with fangs as mustangs pulled wagons driven by monsters to the mound. They unloaded smelly stuff into the cave. No bluff, Saber wanted a muff and it makes my feathers fluff. Later fish popped up dead and dropped again into the bed. Saber stayed in a shiver to keep an eye on the river. I told the puma three bright horses would come and asked him to help some. All nature is ready to give stallions medallions if can stop the deadly battalions."

"I will stop the dastardly rascals," Astro charges.

"Wait! These dangerous chemicals are not our specialty. Strategic humans could help," suggests Spirit.

Scout flies downstream to follow dead fish floating on the river and to warn other creatures not to drink.

Utopio remembers a family, who owns a farm in a nearby meadow explaining, "We will go to the Goodman's' place and put our trust in them."

"Whew! It smells around here. Let's hurry while it is still daylight!" exclaims Astro.

"Right, let's get out of here!

They anxiously canter upriver alongside red cliffs to a draw going up to top land. They gallop over green grassy fields between autumn colored trees to find the Goodman's farm. It rests at the bottom of surrounding hills only a half a day's trek northwest from the spring. The house is a modest ranch-style home situated across a wooden bridge over a wide flowing creek.

Chapter 2

THE RECRUITMENT

Jake Goodman works hard picking apples alongside teenage son Max and hired hand Will Marsh from Plentyville, Beautyland's Capitol. They notice the three steeds approaching.

Jake says, "Welcome, stallions! Max, give them some apples."

"Here you go, a whole bucket, fellas."

Jake asks, "Hey boys, why don't you eat?"

"It looks like they want to tell us something," says Will.

"Look, the big one is rearing and turning, and now the others. They want us to follow. That is Utopio, what are you trying to say, boy? I know that big yellow stallion. I saved him from drowning in the river during a flash flood nineteen years ago. We kept him two or more years. Never could domesticate him. He had a mind of his own, and one day he disappeared," Jake explains.

"Dad, let's follow them," says Max.

"Right, son, go get our rifles and some rope. No telling what is out there, and Will, go saddle our horses! Max, bring Lady! The collie can help track"

The celestial studs understand and eat the apples while waiting.

Mr. Goodman kisses wife Judy, and his youngest child, Kristin, and tells them not to worry before heading out.

"This shouldn't take long but these horses are really fired up. If we are not back by morning, go to Cavanaugh's ranch. It is only a couple of hours ride. Everything will be all right. Utopio and friends probably found another colt in trouble is all. Look at them, they cannot stand still, they want us to hurry."

The strong farmer hugs and kisses Judy goodbye once more.

"The horses are ready," says Will.

"Look at Lady sniffing out the studs," Max replies.

"My horse is the most sure-footed. It's best if I lead," Will exclaims in passing to the position.

They head out in single file behind the supernaturally colored studs toward the spring.

"Whoa, I hear a wagon and some voices," Jake says after a time, in the lead as they approach.

The angelic horses spook and gallop behind boulders on the hillside. The men dismount, tie up under an oak, and listen. Max sneaks up a slope overlooking the monsters and signals to come look. Max holds Lady's mouth shut to keep her from barking. Will holds his mouth shut from yelping. Seven hideous dogs trot in front of wagons driven by large, red and black, furry beasts. They whip four blistered mustangs to pull harder up the path. The wagon creeps along toward the spring carrying potato sacks stuffed with white powder.

Max whispers, "What is going on, Dad? Where did they come from? What are they doing here?"

Jake says, "I don't know, son. We will climb to the top and get a better look. Will, you bring the horses."

"Yes, sir, I'll take them behind the thicket all the way up."

"Max, stay with me. Hold the ammunition. Be careful and watch your step," says Jake.

They crouch low in bushes at the top scrutinizing wagon cargo and Will ties the dobbins nearby.

Jake whispers, "I think the sacks are arsenic. The yellow blocks look worse. I am not sure what any of it is. I smell garlic but if they are going to poison the spring, it can't be.

"Right, what we smell is not arsenic. I think its white phosphorous. The feed store sells arsenic to kill rats. It don't smell like this," Will surmises.

Jake suggests, "Maybe it's arsenic and phosphorous. I know it's deadly, whatever it is."

"There ain't no official labels on those blocks!" Max adds.

Jake explains, "All right son, here is what you're going to do. Ride home fast and ready the weapons for your mother and sister. Tell them to keep the doors and windows locked. Then go to Cavanaugh's place. Tell him to recruit neighbors and follow tracks to whence came. Mention the pit bulls and tell him to 'recon' with an arsenal. He knows how to battle and it may come to that. These are no ordinary foes, Max. Do exactly as I say."

"Yes, Father, I will."

Jake, a retired general, fought with the Continental Army against the invasion by Gejacom. His many victories led to the ultimate freedom Beautyland enjoys today.

"We're going to Plentyville to warn the President. I don't know how long we will be gone," he says.

"I understand, Father. Where is Lady? I want her to come with me."

He answers, "I don't know."

Will says, "I saw her run up the wash after Utopio."

Jake adds, "She will be fine. There is no time to waste. Just get going, Max! Lady will go home when she gets hungry."

"Yes, sir," he answers and leaves in the setting sun.

Jake whispers to Will, "Ride around the mound with me and stay out of sight. Let's look at the river."

"Yes, sir, I brought my Colt if need be.".

"I've got an extra Winchester on my horse and plenty of ammo too," Jake adds.

"How about we just clean them out right now? We can set up an ambush. We don't need any more cause," says Will.

"I tell you, if the Blessing is contaminated then by God as our witness, it's a done deal. Untie the horses. We will walk to those Cedars, mount and ride down the draw, beside the spring. Let's go," Jake exclaims!

At the base of the spring, Will whispers, "The River smells."

"Right, and dead fish. Shish, come here. Listen, do you hear that," asks Jake?

Inside the mound, the foreigners converse in a gruff language. They hear, "Ulandees alang da rivey aete da fisey's ind daud. Oon alie Ulandee's il doy!"

Another voice asks, "Quant eh fiseys en rivey daud?"

The first answers, "Ess, ots fiseys daud!"

"People downstream ate fish and died. Many fish are dead and soon all Beaulancians will die," Jake interprets.

Another one says, "Di ordi onols aves een idiay."

"He said a hoard controls slaves at a base hideout. Wait, I can't hear something about the morning, keep quiet."

Will shrugs having not said anything.

Multiple voices shout, "Beautae ill bae arrs!"

"They say all of Beautyland will be theirs."

Another voice speaks, "Waee ill daetoy dere rop awter witiss sarsnic ee ite osors nda ira wit ilfer ewaksade oontele awle Ulandee's daud."

"That one said, 'It won't be long before the white phosphorus and arsenic in the water and sulfur dioxide in the air kill us. Shish, there's more."

"Blaze ill ake mae orlnel dor is een cuan Ulandees dir dauet ey ordeed."

"And that one said a certain someone named Blaze is going to make him a colonel for this. When all Beaulancians are dead, he'll be glorified. What devils!"

Will whispers, "So we were right and they want to fumigate our air!"

"I studied languages at the academy. That's as close as I can tell," Jake agrees.

Both men shake their heads in grief.

Will remarks, "We have never dealt with anything like this."

"Right, but we can defeat them. Good always conquers evil. Are you ready? Shoot the guard dogs first and draw the others out. If they don't come we will go in and get them. Take no prisoners."

"God help us," Will quietly replies.

He follows Jake to a thicket above the chamber and they pick targets. Scout watches from a tall tree on the ridge. Jake fires his .30-30 and hits a demonic canine in the heart. It falls spilling out steaming tar, shakes it off and gets up.

"Get the horses," shouts Jake!

Will was already gone and rides up leading Jake's horse. He jumps on as the wounded dog leaps. The horse swerves and dodges. The hound protrudes long metal fangs out a hot fuming mouth and tries again.

The frightened horse cuts direction saving its throat. The hound lands spiked chompers on Jake's canteen. Water bursts out immediately squirting it like quenching fire." The jackal falls with fangs withered by mere water drops from a canteen. His body sizzles and his fiery eyes are burnt out as he falls dead with steam puffing out his mouth like a teakettle. It keels over melting into red-hot sludge and then the glow of hot coals diminishes. The beast's eyes have turned into empty black sockets!

The men lose thoughts in racing away to reach the plateau before any other surprises. Once there, they stop for words.

"Jake, I've never been so scared."

"You never so scared, that creature bit at me. I have never seen anything with metal teeth. It was a devil of a beast. Did you watch it die? My punctured canteen slightly dripped and the freakish mutt died like heated boysenberry syrup."

"Yes sir, and I saw your shot too! The bullet made a hole directly through its heart and the dang thing got up as good as new. A touch of water instantly killed it. Is the pup made of fire?"

"If it came from the underworld then I suppose so," Jake replies.

"A creature burning inside out ain't like nothing I ever seen before. We're lucky we didn't have to contend with the big wagon drivers," says Will.

"Yeah, they could pass for gorillas with all of that fur."

"Or bears maybe but did you notice a human resemblance in their faces," asks Will?

"I didn't get that good a look. I was more concerned about the cargo. I imagine I'll get another chance. What about their faces?"

"Oh, I don't know but the nose on one I seen weren't like a bear nor a gorilla. Did you notice their heads had bangs over eyes and long hair over ears?"

"I did see heads full of hair blowing in the wind," Jake answers.

"Have you ever heard of 'Living Water'," asks Will?

"Sure, it is the symbol of protecting grace."

"Your water was the living end with graceful protection and sure put the mutt out fast, didn't it?" He rhetorically asks.

Jake says, "You said it! Water is our weapon of choice. I bet it works on all those monsters. This really enlightens the situation and gives me ideas."

Will asks, "What ya thinking about?"

"Well, I'm not quite ready to explain, but a plan is brewing. There are still just too many unanswered questions. I'll analyze everything along the way. Don't worry you'll be the first to know if any bright ideas come to mind. It's getting dark. We can't ride all night. We should camp between here and the Capital. Stay alert for a good spot and watch for trouble."

Will says in jest, "My canteen is full!"

"Seriously, I wish I had a barrelful of water right now," says Jake.

Will remarks, "Don't fret sir, strong protection watches over us!"

Jake silently wonders about this so-called Blaze person. Will silently prays for strong, strong, protection thinking, *"Why would he want to cause so much damage?*

In sizing up the situation, Jake suddenly explodes with,

"The dastardly beings, what kind of creatures purposely and chemically destroy land and water? Everything would shrivel up and die and for what cause? Are we Beaulancians extinguishable? We must defeat them with no holds barred. These marauders are crazy about killing our environment."

Great stress wears on the men riding through forestland at night.

Chapter 3

THE WEAPONRY

The scared riders move through Plenty Territory listening to crackling leaves and watching shooting stars. The night invokes solemn retrospect with weariness encouraging food cravings when suddenly Jake sees a distant firelight.

"Will, do you see what I see?"

"I do."

"Someone set a cozy camp under those Sequoias. We will blend in behind and see if they are friendly. Maybe we could invite ourselves for a warm-up at the fire. If neighborly, we might get some good grub. What do you say, Will?"

"I never look a gift horse in the mouth. It is worth a try."

As Jake gets closer, he sees Takoda. The men have been friends since childhood. Takoda's mother helped deliver Jake at birth. They occasionally hunt and fish together. Takoda has another special friend sitting with him beside the fire. In fact, he is petting him while chanting a soothing lullaby. It is a Sabor Toes, the puma.

Jake points the lion to Will and calls with a mockingbird whistle to Takoda asking, "Hey, brother, got room for two more?"

Takoda stands saying, "Welcome my brother, come and sit."

"Uh, what about that cat, should I ready my rifle?" asks Jake.

Takoda says, "No, Kamawawby, Saber Toes wouldn't hurt anybody, not the good ones anyway. Sit down. There is much to eat. I catch many fish today."

They dismount and walk their nervous mounts into camp as Saber Toes departs into the forest.

"Fish, huh, Takoda, where did you catch those fish?" Jake asks.

"Elk Pond, largemouth bass, good bass, take some," he says.

Jake explains, "We are on our way to Plentyville. We found alien fiends dumping poison in the Blessing. Dead fish are popping up like bubbles on spear grass. Have you eaten any of that fish yet? We heard a demon talk of folks eating poisoned fish and dying. They purposely contaminated the river."

Will adds, "Right, many farmers and ranchers died," he said. We just had the scare of our lives when a demonic dog attacked us at the spring. One-man-beast said other poisons would come down from the air and kill everyone off. They are sabotaging Beautyland. We have to spread the word and recruit help. Takoda defensive actions are mandatory. This is no joke. So, have you eaten any of that fish yet?"

Takoda nods and says, "Good fish!"

Jake asks, "Are you sure you feel all right?"

Takoda answers, "Yes, brother, I am good. Here you eat some. It is good fish."

Jake grabs one by the middle, smells it and then chomps down with unafraid hunger. It tastes great, boneless and spicy. Will gets a fish from the hot pan saying, "Emm, this is good. I need another piece."

"I see dog beast. Saber come and take me to charcoaled dog. It hangs from notched cliff with eyeholes wide-open and eyeballs gone. Sabertoes scratches go deep into dogs face, nothing but darkness inside wounds. Saber gouged eyes but burnt claw. It bother him, I treat it," says Takoda.

"The dog had long fangs, right? It probably stood three feet high and four feet long. It was red and muscular with black ears and one red sock on a hind leg with black socks on the others, right?" Jake asks.

"It was burnt inside out. I could not tell its colors," Takoda replies.

"I shot ones heart out and it would not die. It came after me, but the stupid devilish thing missed and bit my canteen. The water spewed and killed it like quenching a fire," says Jake.

Takoda points, exclaiming, "See glowing horse prints over there, three sets, Kamawawby!"

"Right! One is Utopio, a magnificent stallion with two other very special studs from Folkhaven. The ground radiates where they stand. They roused us to the spring. They knew something was up. They wanted to warn us. Could you pass the fish?" asks Jake.

"I'm hungrier than a lost alligator myself, all right if I have some more?" Will then asks.

"There is plenty so eat and get strong!" Takoda exclaims.

They silently pause while looking at the fire and absorb the past conversation for new ideas.

Jake says, "Well, at least the fish in Elk Pond are pure. My belly knows that. Listen Takoda, keep out of sight with an eye on the river and warn any person seen not to eat from or near it. If you see anything suspicious, get up atop Mount Harmony and send smoke signals. We will watch from our way to Plentyville. Use one puff at a time between pauses if you see the enemy. Make a steady stream if you need help and get out of there. Send three quick puffs at a time if trouble is coming our way. Bring plenty of water and if you get in a fix squirt your canteen at the enemy."

"The varmints might die if you shoot their eyes out. It is worth a try if need be. Better yet, use wet arrows and then go away fast on your paint," says Will.

"That is the main thing, brother. Do not let them get you. Have you got it?" asks Jake.

"I will do as you say, my brother," Takoda replies.

"Then we'll be on our way. Thanks for the chow!"

"Yes, thanks, Takoda. Good to meet you, you are a mighty fine cook, my friend. Watch your back, I hope to fish with you when this is all over. Goodbye," Will wishes.

Four miles later, the pair approaches a farmhouse. They dismount and tie up to a hitching post before the front porch. They cautiously knock on a loose front door and wait two minutes without a reply. Jake walks around back and finds a conspicuous plow near the barn but the barn is empty. He goes to get a better look and sure enough no horse or animals are anywhere in sight.

Will walks around the side and sees a pie on an open kitchen window and a lit lantern in the main room. Together they knock at the back door. After only a minute without answer, they check the barn again. It is definitely empty but persistent Will finds unharmed chickens behind it.

Jake goes around to another side and says, "Will, look here!"

"Dagnab it, look at that pooch. The poor fella has burn holes the size of lemons between his ears. General, we better go inside the house and look around."

Jake says, "You can help me break in if needed but let's try the knob first. It is open. Look, there are dog tracks all over the hardwood floors."

"I see beds for seven. A big family must live here," says Will.

"Take a look at this footprint. I never saw one like this from a person," says Jake.

"No not anyone, dang it's a big one. It has large width but it's short in length," Will responds.

Jake adds, "What's that on the wood floor in front of the prints? Are those toenail scratches? The depths of the marks look very dangerous. Can you see how deep in the grain they go?"

"Every step is the same. When this thing walks, it grabs. Its toes are bent. That is why the deep scratches," adds Will.

"No signs of a scuffle, other than the curled rug, and no signs of blood. Everything looks intact. We had better get a move on," says Jake.

Will agrees, exclaiming, "Let's fill canteens at the well and be off!"

"You go on and do it. I want to study the grounds just a bit more before we leave."

Will unties the horses and leads them to a spigot about thirty feet from the house. Jake scopes out the property under moonlit skies.

"Jake! This water is no good. We *Kaint* drink it!" yells Will.

A full bucket sits on the well housing's wooden ledge and a dead bird floats on top.

Jake runs over, looks in, and says, "The bird didn't drown, its feathers singed, look at those hollow eyes, it drank poisoned water."

Then he notices beastly tracks beside two dog prints.

"There is a horse with them. A plow horse I bet. They are headed east toward the spring," observes Will.

"Look, white powder spots beside wagon ruts going west. If we follow I bet we'll find the folks," says Jake.

"Jake, what are we going to do about more water? From here to Plentyville, the river is polluted and I imagine more wells are too!"

Jake says, "Right Will I understand. Hmm, a quarter mile up the foothills of Mount Harmony, the glacier snow ought to be good. It is very cold. I think the hot-blooded creatures would smolder there. The snowmelt could sustain us."

"Good thinkin', sir! It is another hundred miles to the Capitol and we need water. It is worth the chance. We can fill our canteens, water the horses, and get down the buffalo trail to the valley. We may reach Plentyville in two and a half days if we hurry."

"Right Will, but we'd better commandeer some warm coats hanging on the wall in the house. I'll grab a few and some more blankets."

"And some canned food too, sir!"

Heading out, they notice crushed pecans around tracks.

Jake says, "The family left markers through this orchard and alfalfa bends flat against the dirt just past those trees."

They follow human tracks carefully over broken soil. Short and wide monster feet with deep toenail imprints walk on each side of the human prints.

Will says, "Fifty beasts and thirty dogs head to Plentyville. Distinctively different pointed boot prints lead the pack. Farmer boot prints walk along in all sizes, adult and children."

"These beast prints in the front are following in double file. There is too many for us to fight. We need water," says Jake.

"We ought to look around the farm for canteens," Will suggests.

"Good idea, hurry on then," says Jake.

They kick into a gallop to search the house and find no canteens. The barn renders only a useless punctured one.

"Now what," asks Will?

Jake says, "Buckets are no good. I don't know."

Will says, "That dog of theirs was a big dog, maybe a Saint Bernard. Folks around here use them for search and rescue. Saint Bernard's carry whiskey barrels around their necks to use on injuries."

"Right, let's look," says Jake.

"Yep, maybe there is a complete harness around here," he agrees.

"We never checked the cellar. Let us look down there," says Jake.

They go behind the house and open two halves of a slanted wooden cellar door beside the kitchen entry. Stairs lead down to a large storage room filled with nuts, potatoes, and grain barrels. They find old clothes, toys, hand tools, small crates of personal items, and junk in general. Will grabs an old potato sack and fills it with oatmeal, potatoes, and pecans. Jake finds shelves and hooks against the far wall.

He says, "Eureka! Here it is, just like we thought a three gallon whiskey barrel and four empty wineskins too!"

Will looks them over and says, "Hey! We can fill these skins and squeeze 'em. I bet they squirt twenty feet."

"We can make them to, if they don't!" Jake exclaims.

They tie the skins and the barrel to their ponies and leave with a new confidence. There is no time to lose in getting up to colder land and pure mountain streams.

Chapter 4

GOODMAN'S SANCTUARY

Currently, Mr. Cavanaugh will not leave his son alone this night to round up neighbors. He listens to the dubious dispatch from Max and tells him to go home. At dawn, he will undertake the task.

Instead of going home directly, Max keeps his mother and sister up all night with worry. He wanders the land searching for Lady. At one point, he saw her. Now he travels a dark ravine twenty miles from the Spring of Plenty where wolves howl and owls whoop. Nothing else stirs in the night. Daisy, a sure-footed palomino walks carefully in and out of the sandy ravine. Max's eyes strain to see anything in the dark. This is dangerous territory and the rustic country boy knows not to push his horse or let her run away with him.

Realizing the futility of riding in darkness, he dismounts, ties Daisy to a juniper tree and puts a feed sack of oats around her nose. He builds a small fire and heats up some jarred pinto beans with ham hocks and molasses. He calls out Lady's name through the darkness nineteen miles from where she ran away at the spring. He keeps warm by the fire hoping she went home with reason to believe she did not. He thinks she followed Utopio running after something not away from anything. Then suddenly Daisy alarms him with a loud whinny. Lady is stretching in a fast run up the ravine only several hundred feet away leading Utopio, Spirit and Astro.

Max shouts, "She heard me, Daisy! She heard me. Come on, Lady, come here, girl, come on!"

Soon Lady and the studs run past. He quickly steps around Daisy to mount and says, "Oh no I forgot to untie you girl!"

She rears and breaks the branch holding tied reins. Max grabs it as she scoots back, untangles and leaps on kicking out fast after Lady.

Snarling dogs chase. The front-runner is none other than Lucer. He is the meanest most beastly bred jackal, Blaze Evil ever trained. Purple lava drools over platinum teeth. His tongue spits steamy oozing blobs twenty feet at the escaping party. Four other bad-to-the-bone mongrels follow Lucer.

Utopio stops to block attacks as Lady slows closer to Max. He knocks two hounds thirty feet into the air with dynamic kicks. Lucer stops in surprise to see what he does next allowing Max to catch Lady leaping for his lap. He straddles her over the mare's neck and leaves the ravine at a full run up a ridge. They move around a sharp curve and down a canyon slope toward home.

The studs guard and detour the dogs away from the farm. It is Max's only shelter for miles.

He hollers, "Follow me, Utopio, yee-ha!"

They run splashing through a wide creek twelve miles east of Cavanaugh's place. Astro crosses last and notices the ghoulish dogs stop two hundred feet before the creek. He wonders all the way to the Goodman's farm why they gave up. Judy waits anxiously on the front porch. Max goes directly to the barn, brushes down all four horses and puts them away with feed in stalls.

The celestial ones have never been in an earth barn together and they love it. The stalls have a cozy warm feel with cedar shavings on the floor and all the alfalfa they can eat. The small water troughs in each stall are good and so are the salt blocks. Their new friend Daisy is a beautiful sight to boot.

Lady and Max are in the five-room house. It has three bedrooms, a family room and a kitchen, complete with rations on the floor for Lady. The table is set with food for Max. The family room has a sofa, three chairs and a corner pillow for Lady. Judy is there, giving Max a tongue-lashing. Kristin quietly listens from the kitchen dining table. She smiles with gladness for their safe return and his being in trouble. Max spends the next hour explaining. Afterwards he gets the guns ready at the table while eating.

Judy says, "You wait until your father comes home and learns you went looking for Lady instead of coming right home. Why are you cleaning the guns at the table?"

He says, "All is well, Mom. I am home now so get some sleep. I have to do this somewhere. I am hungry."

Everyone deals differently with this anxiety until finally retiring at 4:00 a.m. to save strength. Judy thanks God before shutting her eyes saying, "Home by two thirty in the morning is better than not at all. Thank you God and please help his father and Will. Thank you, God. Amen."

Daisy and the unusual steeds mingle in the barn with the regular inhabitants, including Violet, a glossy black horse, Danny Boy, a red draft horse with a flaxen yellow mane and long, tall Freckles, a creamy strawberry roan. Mirabelle, the milk cow; five sheep; two goats, and a rabbit named Pop-Up. All listen with cautious eyes to these three lustrous visitors. Their open-mouthed stares do not intimidate the angelic horses. Most strangers react the same way when Utopio flares his red tail and mane. His predominantly yellow body has a few red bands running along conforming muscles. His sleek conformation is very strong and athletic. Yellow and red halos gleam over his proud stature like neon lights. The brothers Spirit and Astro display predominantly yellow coats. Multicolored overlapping fibers emit green and purple halos. Their manes and tails are bright fluorescent blue as are parts of their backs and legs.

Danny Boy finally speaks to Utopio, asking, "I know you, do I not?"

Utopio says, "Of course you do. I lived here; remember when I followed you in the field? You plowed a perfect row. I kicked the dirt back into the trench. You said that if I kept it up…"

Danny Boy interrupts to finish the statement with "You'll be lying in that bed you are making. Hahaha."

Utopio answers, "Yep, you remember alright! I never forgot you either. I wondered if you had changed. I can see by your great laugh that you have not. It is good to see you again, my golden mane friend. I have missed you."

"You look good too, Utopio. Life on the freedom trail is nice, huh?"

"Truly it is all good, Danny Boy. One day you will be on it with me. I am sure you will see for yourself someday. Allow me to introduce my cousins, Spirit and Astro! These comely studs taught me much about myself. The two of them found me after I departed from here and the adventures have never stopped. I was wandering alone on a faraway mesa, trying to find the valley. They appeared on a ledge as I attempted down a jagged cliff. Spirit asked what I thought I was doing. Well, I said, 'I am going down this ram trail.' Together they showed me an amazing power I had forgotten I had. When I entered the atmosphere coming to this paradise I had forgotten whom I was. It was like being born again!"

Daisy asks, "Power, what power?"

Then Violet asks, "You have a power?"

Astro says, "He sure does, and so do we."

Danny Boy asks, "Well, what is this power?"

"Topio, shall I tell them?" Astro asks.

Topio says, "No, okay, I will. The fact is that it is a power we use sparingly. We all have been blessed with magical hair."

Astro interjects, "See, I am floating."

His tail, mane, and hooves fan out holding his weight above the ground like wings. He defies gravity and Spirit joins in to do the same. Finally, Utopio spreads out his lustrous extensions and floats.

"Wow!" Mirabelle mutters.

Then Freckles asks, "Can you fly?"

"We can, somewhat and it sure helps to get to the top or bottom of a cliff," Utopio insists.

Then Astro says, "We can zoom over tall trees and reach the tops of high mesas in a single bound."

Daisy's eyes glisten with romantic feelings as she asks Utopio, "What else can you do?"

Looking back at her with a gulp in his throat, he answers proudly, "I can ricochet a bullet off any part of my diamond carbonic fibrous mass. I can stand in fire indefinitely without burns. I retain the almighty gift of illusionism. I can appear as something I am not, if need be."

Spirit concurs, "He is indeed endowed with this ability."

Astro prods Topio and says, "Go on and show them something."

Spirit incites him to do a burning bush and warns everyone.

"Now, remember this is not real. Do not be afraid."

The frightening imitation begins. Utopio wraps his red tail around his body and waves his mane. He tucks his head under his breast and the legs go underneath, putting his belly on the ground. The imposing array of reds and yellows nearly cause a stampede as Freckles shouts, "Fire, help, fire, help, help, fire!"

The animals burst into a jumping frenzy.

Astro says, "It's not real, it's not real, be still."

Spirit says, "Topio, snap out of it before they bust the doors down."

First, he laughs into a roll on the hay-covered floor, and then Topio gets up and apologizes for the scare. He assures them they were never in any danger.

"It's just me. Can you see me Daisy? Open your eyes. Go ahead and touch. It will not hurt. I promise. I am not even hot."

Relieved animal sounds fill the room.

Danny Boy says, "I think I have seen enough for one night. I really cannot believe my eyes. Thank you very much. It was quite a show, Topio."

The others remain speechless. Utopio bows to cover his reddened face and says, "It has been good to meet everyone. We should get some sleep now. Good night, all."

His two partners gather around and they lie down together in a large soft stall shutting their eyes for the night.

At first light, Daisy enters the open stall with her white-snipped nose and tells Utopio how much she enjoyed the performance.

She asks, "Where are you from?"

He nods and replies, "Another dimension, I am from an existence within your own. One day you all will live in my world with the greatest power of all the universes. Someday, not now, but you will come and see my place, one day! I am sure!"

Spirit overhears and redirects Daisy's eyes out an open window steering her glance upward toward Folkhaven. He explains to her with special attraction as a gentle and mature middle-aged stallion, "That is where we are all from, pretty Daisy. We are here to complete a mission. Yesterday, we had no idea what it was, but now we know."

Daisy asks, "What is it?"

Utopio takes over and explains, "An old enemy of the Beaulancian King, 'Harmonious the Great,' from long ago, has returned trying to dominate Beautyland. Our calling is to obstruct and dispose of him for all time."

Danny Boy lifts his head over the stall and asks, "How do you know this? Who is this enemy?"

Astro steps near and explains, "Yesterday evening we saw him. The Evil one was talking to his notorious dog Lucer and no one of Beautyland is a match for those two. His evil dog gang chased us for hours until finally they stopped as we crossed the creek."

Violet asks, "Who is Evil?"

Spirit says, "I shall tell you! Gather around everyone for a history lesson. Blaze Evil has always been a thief and a killer."

Chapter 5

HERITAGE

S pirit starts the lesson by explaining, "Long, long ago, great immorality afflicted Beautyland. This villain sought to overtake all that was good and caring. King Harmonious, being a wise and courageous monarch, petitioned Folkhaven to rid the kingdom of his wickedness. One day, while seeking a secluded place away from the guarded palace for prayer and meditation, he found the Spring of Plenty. There before his eyes the hand of God touched the spring and blessed it as a refreshing source for all living creatures. Even now, we know it as from an aquifer of Living Water. The king fell to his knees and cried out with thanks and praise singing, 'Alleluia, Lord!' God confirmed to him that the land would return to its previous decency. The spring symbolized purification.

"Then suddenly flashing down from the forest above, a messenger horse appeared. This miraculous mare is a great ancestor of Utopio. Her name is Bandy for passing 'to and fro.' She is white with beautiful red bands marking a perfect body, similar to Utopio.

"Anyway, she bowed before the king and gave him special instructions to move his family and all the virtuous subjects into the caverns of the spring. He must collect two domestic creatures of every kind, male and female, two wild creatures of every kind, male and female. He shall gather the crawly kind and the flying kind. The directive warned him to bring enough food for all to feed on for more than a year. She advised him to seal the cave except for a small eyehole. Soon ferocious winds would roar and carry the malicious creatures out to sea. Bandy instructed that when the winds ceased, Harmonious was to send an eagle through the hole to scour the kingdom until it was certain that all the evil creatures were gone.

"Blaze overheard while squatting under a large evergreen bush nearby. However, his slyness did not conceal him from the Sovereign Power above. He and his accomplices were to soon deal with wrath. Royal Harmonious did exactly as Bandy had instructed.

"And having heard the plan, Blaze, who is very evil, gathered his cronies and quickly built a haphazard sailing vessel from gopher wood. They loaded it with supplies and sailed away in the winds to escape. Aboard were some evil female concubines and nine evil jackals. There were three males and six females. There were rations enough for all and many other two-footed, demonic scoundrel accomplices.

"Winds furiously blew them away from Beautyland. The craft rocked and tossed through mountainous waves, which soon separated its unsealed joints. The turbulence kept them rousing from side to side and bailing constantly for forty days and forty nights. Seasickness, fear and clamor gripped them. Blaze tyrannically ruled meandering on choppy ocean waters for fifteen months.

"Meanwhile, Harmonious saw the end of wind and rain through the lookout hole. He prompted the eagle out to search the land. Twice the eagle returned, unsure of any survivors. On the third trip, however, he brought back a live groundhog in his claws. This signified the land was dry, to come out without fear of flood. They all considered the wretched Evil ones had perished. Therefore, King Harmonious, his wife, three sons, two daughters, friends, good neighbors, townsfolk and creatures exited the hollow ground. They multiplied and the King trustworthy led in prospering their lineage unto this day.

"As for the wrongdoers, during tribulation the turbulent water continued until finally crashing onto a rocky shore. Their vessel was broken into pieces. It was a remote Island having only volcanos living there. Now shipwrecked but alive, these ghastly fiends discovered their new homeland. It has been a safe distance away for eons and a wretched barren place for the survivors. Even so, upon landing one of Blaze's favorite maidens whooped loudly with optimism, 'What a relief!'

"Blaze felt the same way and decreed the island, Relief Island. They clung in safety to its dry rocky land as a big blue whale rose speaking a dispatch from the omnipotent Supreme Being.

"It said, 'Now, hear this. So you think that you will like it here, do you? Take notice, except for volcanos and sulfur springs, this zone is bare. Under hot inverted cones, you shall dwell for eons. The center of the earth with fire and gas shall be your quarters. Nutrients you shall find in molten lava! To quench thirst, seek the sulfur springs. As punishment for heinous murders, thefts, greediness, assaults, deceptions, and hate, you shall drink sour, warm and smelly, polluted liquids filled with metals. Anything unfit for any other life will be your staple. Contact with waters insufficient in sulfur, or fresh, clean and pure, shall readily end your lives. This is your sentence. This curse shall carry forward to future generations.

"All accomplices around the universe shall be delivered to crowd your endurance. Avoid these warnings and you shall perish. Your existence depends on it. You will live here or die. You applaud idolatry, treachery, debauchery, torture, murder, and much more. You refuse repentance and previous false penances have not justified your acts. Sorrow is beneath you. Hence, your judgment exists. You need not obey. Your death is my preference," said the whale!

Spirit continues, "Lizards basking everywhere on the island lifted their heads up and stuck their drooling tongues out. The message was noted as the whale blasted a stream out his air hole. The evils ran. If the water had hit any of them it would have killed them. He then submerged beneath the sea up to an exposed eye winked and dipped fully out of sight under the ocean. Their fate was foretold and this is why to this day they will not step into a stream."

Utopio says, "Blaze wears a black cape, and has red-and-black hair. We saw him yesterday with his most evil demon dog, Lucer. It was surely Blaze Evil or someone who looked exactly like him. Somehow, he has returned as though the island was not far enough away to hold him."

Astro says, "We know he is poisoning the Blessing. We witnessed a beast's death by water. It was a terrorizing type of dog. It jumped at Mr. Goodman and pierced his canteen. The dog died from only draining water."

Utopio says, "Will and Jake got away unharmed. We hid behind boulders in a gulch and saw them pollute the river.

Spirit says, "They whipped captured mustangs and plow horses into hauling means of destruction. We watched them dump a wagon full of poisons into hoppers over a furnace. They heated it into an elixir and ran the liquid down spouts into the river."

Astro says, "It smells like garlic and rotten eggs. The furnace emits dangerous gases. We gagged and held our breaths. Lucer saw us spying and chased us here."

Danny Boy reacts emotionally but patriotically ready to defend. He says, "What the heck, I mean where the heck, I mean what is this heck, and where do I fight it? Whatever you want me to do I am in for it. I will kick a dog three hundred yards. I will stomp a demon flat with my left front hoof. I can whip a demons head off with my tail. I will bite arms and legs in two with one chomp. Where do you need me, Topio? I am enlisting!"

Then Violet steps up and says, "Fighting terrorists, trying to destroy our land, oh yeah, boys, count me in!"

Spirit accepts their enlistment and recommends all animals follow in national defense. The barn is loud with discussions of invasion defeating strategy.

Judy and Kristin are in the kitchen preparing batter for hotcakes and other breakfast goodies. Max is putting the guns in easy to reach places around the living room. Even in expecting another eventful day only the usual morning grumblings about chores and lack of sleep

32

bounce through the house. Judy sets a large platter of eggs, biscuits, bacon, fried potatoes, and a jar of homemade jelly on the table. Kristin adds a platter of fresh hot cakes, a jug of their own maple syrup, and a tub of butter. Max sets coffee cups and glasses of farm-picked apple juice down. Judy comes again with salt, pepper, cream, napkins, and silverware. Lady eats leftover stew and corn bread from the night before on the front porch. All the Goodman family except Jake takes places at the table.

They eat only after offering thanks to God for their safety and other blessings. The table talk focuses on routine chores. They selflessly control inner worries to avoid depressing themselves.

Max says, "I will feed the animals, clean the stable, chop wood, patch the roof and clean the fireplace before noon."

Judy says, "I'll have more in mind after lunch. Kristin, you pick apples, de-shell pecans, scrub the floors, and pluck a chicken. I will busy myself cleaning the kitchen, mending clothes, ironing, and preparing lunch."

Her long blonde hair conceals concerned blue eyes. Kristin looks similar to Judy as she notices her mother's trembling hand lift a coffee cup.

"Mother, are you all right?" she asks.

Since hearing Jake heads to Plentyville, she assumes all responsibility as the only guardian and it disturbs her.

She says, "I am a bit tired, honey!"

Max finishes eating quietly and thanks them for breakfast. He excuses himself to work in the barn. Kristin helps clear the table.

She asks, "Mom, why do you think these creatures are poisoning the river?"

Judy answers, "One can only guess why anyone would go to such lengths. I wish I knew."

Max overhears and says, "Everything will be fine. It's only man beasts with brutally ugly dogs."

Kristin asks, "From where they came I'd like to know?"

Judy says, "From somewhere far, far away, not from Beautyland. I hope Dad is careful. He gets aggressive without thinking sometimes."

Kristin says, "But only for goodness' sake. He is always aware of everything."

Max says, "He tore the Gejacom's to shreds before I was born."

Judy hands Kristin a wet dish, adding, "Here, I'll wash, and you dry."

"Mom, you're crying," says Kristin.

Max says, "Dad is a brilliant general. He knows what he is doing."

Judy says, "I guess I shouldn't worry so much. You are right Max dear. We were losing that war until he came along."

Max says, "He'll do it again. He will crush 'em. Just wait and see."

Kristin says, "He is the best!"

In that instant, Kristin cuts her finger on a sharp knife and squeals. Judy grabs a clean napkin and wraps the wound.

She says, "Sit down and hold the cloth on it until it stops bleeding. I will finish the dishes. When the bleeding stops, put your gloves on and go pick apples, honey. I want to make a pie today so pick the best ones. Get a couple of baskets for cider and some to treat the horses."

Kristin says, "We should jar some applesauce while we're at it."

Judy answers, "Sure, sweetheart, we can do that, but you might have to pick an extra basket."

Kristin says, "Right, okay, Mom, no problem."

Judy says, "It's such a beautiful day. I'll patch Dad's britches on the porch."

Chapter 6

UNITED

Lady runs from the chicken coop barking at coming horses. Judy stops sewing the pants and stands. Kristin hears trotting hooves and runs out to the porch. Max is in the barn.

Charlie Cavanaugh approaches, shouting, "Hello, Judy! We wanted to check on you before going any further. You know marksmen Hank Johnson, Ben Reed, and sure-shooting Molly Hastings."

Judy replies, "Of course I do, howdy everyone!"

Charlie says, "They're armed, ready, and willing to take on anything."

Judy says, "I am so glad you came by. We are fine, just a bit worried. I feel so much better seeing you, would you like some coffee or how about some breakfast?"

Hank says, "Oh, no, thank you, Ma'am. We ate in the saddle."

Charlie says, "We only stopped by to see what we might do for you."

Molly asks, "Are you sure you're all right, honey?"

Judy says, "Oh yes, we are fine, nothing happening here. We're ready if they come this way, but I know you'll stop 'em!"

"Well, we'll get going then, Jude," says Charlie.

"We will relay Intel to Jake in Plentyville. Is there anything you want us to tell him for you?" asks Ben.

"We love him!" says Judy.

"We will follow tracks at the spring from the eastern crossing. It is a hard story to understand and will not be over 'til it's over, Jude," says Charlie.

Hank says, "take precautions, darlin'."

Molly says, "That's right! Kristin, you help your mother, honey! Do not roam off anywhere. Demons are on the loose."

"That's right! I know your father. When he calls for us, it is a sober summons. He ain't one to play with people," says Charlie.

"You can bet your bottom dollar on that," Molly replies!

Charlie says, "Don't leave home, Judy and keep the kids close. All is well for now, but keep your weapons loaded. If need be, hide in the cellar."

"I mean to tell you, not to be overly fearful, but are you well armed?" asks Hank.

Judy replies, "Oh yes, we are well armed!"

Charlie says, "My place is farther from the spring. If you want, go there anytime. It is likely safer. The rock house is nearly impenetrable and my son Thomas is keeping an eye on the place. Judy, you hear me, he will take you all in."

"Thank you dearly, Charlie," she responds.

He turns to the daughter asking, "Kristin, how are you holding up, Hun?"

He has always thought well of her and seventeen-year-old Thomas really likes her.

She says, "I'm doing fine, sir."

"What is that on your hand?" he asks.

"Oh, it is nothing; I got a little too careless while doing the dishes is all."

"I see. . . Well peace, be with you Goodman's and I am sure, the saboteur is going to regret, ever coming here. We will put them to rest soon. Remember though, be watchful."

Ben asks, "Where's Max?"

Kristin answers, "Oh, he is cleaning up the barn."

Charlie says, "So he did get home safely then, that's good. Your father will be back as soon as possible don't get discouraged. Keep your wits about you, all right, Judy?"

She nods and says, "Charlie, Max was chased last night to the creek by a wild pack of dogs."

"We saw the tracks. Stay ready for anything Judy I am sorry we cannot stay. Go to my house the back way. It will be safer there. I know this is not comforting but it is all I can say, darlin'," he replies.

He salutes her and the others wave a sorry goodbye. They turn into a hurried lope shouting "Viva Beautyland."

Max comes out of the barn watching all the way walking to the porch saying, "They packed enough weapons and tools. Did you notice their bulging saddlebags, Mom?"

"Well, dear, that's a good thing, no telling what's needed. You go on about your chores now and I'm going to finish my sewing."

Judy is quietly more worried now than ever. She sits down on the porch swing in silent prayer.

Kristin decides to visit the colorful horses in the barn on her way to the orchard.

"What dazzling specimens," she says to Max. He loads a shovelful of manure into a cart and asks, "Are the colorful stallions related to each other, do you think?"

"Their markings are very similar, probably so," she says.

Kristin reaches out to pet Astro with her good hand. It contented him, so she puts her sore one around him and hugs his brightly colored neck. A pain-relieving sensation runs throughout her body.

"What was that?" she yelps.

Astro smiles and Max returns the question: "What was what?"

Kristin screams after removing her finger bandage.

Max shouts, "What's wrong?"

"My finger, look at my finger," she says.

Staring at an unmarked normal finger suggests something is wrong with Kristin's head.

"Well, what about it?" he asks.

"Don't you see my perfect index finger? Can't you see the smooth clean skin?"

Max says, "Kristin, aren't you a bit vainly preoccupied here?"

Kristin responds, "No! There was a deep knife wound. I cut it wide open. The sore is completely gone. Why do you think I had this bandage on, dummy? Look at it now, not even a scar!"

Max presses her finger. "Where did it go?"

She says, "I touched his blue mane and the pain left me! Then I took the bandage off and *poof,* no more slit. Here, if you do not believe me, look at the bandage. See the blood stain?"

Nevertheless, Max remains skeptical returning to chores with propounding thoughts saying, "Amazing," and opens the barn door wide pushing the full wheelbarrow. The angelic steeds rush out. Utopio looks around as Kristin runs after. There is no time for sentiment. Judy waves goodbye from the porch, and Max stands still outside the barn with his mouth open. The steeds burst across the property line disappearing quickly. Kristin remains excited about the healing and runs up the porch to her mother saying "Mom, Mom, you will never guess what just happened!"

Chapter 7

THE ARMORY

Merging across the swift Blessing River following wagon tracks near the spring slows the colorful horses down. Six villainous jackals pop out from behind boulders on the bank and six more wait on the opposite side. The horses are stuck in the middle of the river. The beast's growl and slobber red steaming drool off mean toothy jaws. Spirit slides off the slick bottom and goes under. He lifts his legs to float and Utopio says, "Grab my tail."

Spirit presses lips hard with no pressure from teeth and then Astro slips up to his withers but firmly catches Spirit's tail. Utopio pulls both to the bank. More angry mutts are waiting. Astro shakes his illustrious coat and splatters five. They drop to the ground and melt into boiling orange lava. Another dark mongrel locks its fangs onto his dry neck.

He spins 360 degrees shouting, "Bad dog, let go of me!"

It hangs on swinging in midair. Utopio flicks his dripping tail and kills it and several others on both sides of the river. The one on Astro loses grip and falls to the ground. Utopio places a hoof on its smoldering hind, bites its ears and pulls it off. Astro bleeds bright purple from the torn flesh.

He says, "Thanks, Topio, he caused my first ever sore throat! Watch this, I will show that dangly, fangy mutt."

His nimble wet legs kick the unsightly creature fusing into a cactus.

Once Utopio confirms his sidekicks are fine and no other jackals follow, he asserts, "Let's keep moving and find out where these creeps are coming from."

"Definitely, let's go this way," says Spirit.

The remaining beasts on the spring side of the river clamor as the victor's gallop away following wagon tracks. After only a mile past, Astros injury is fully self-healed. The jolly steed sings a ballad for all to hear:

"The gruesome pitiful jackals thought we would drown but only the dopey sludge heads went down. Special Forces are we three and we will never lose peace, love, or tranquility. Against all evil whose victims lay, we will meet the day. We save grotto's singing mottos.

"O Beautyland, O Beautyland, for you with love we make a stand. We fight, O Beautyland, O Beautyland and strike, until we win. They will meet a dreadful end, da-dun, da-dun, and da-dun-dun-dun.

"We will fight the bushwhackers until Beautyland has won. We will fight where they are and where they run. Our victory will surely knock the Blazes done, dadun-dadun!"

Spirit responds, "Sing it like it is."

Utopio notices an intersecting trail saying, "The high mesa is over there."

Spirit says, "Yes, cousin and this road goes to the coast."

They quickly gallop to the crossing. Footprints of man-beasts, dog impressions, and other horse prints clutter the ground.

Topio adds, "It appears the wagons stopped here from all directions. One route goes southeast to the coast and the other heads west toward Plentyville."

Analytical Spirit wonders why both paths begin and end at a lonely hillside bush. He searches the area for clues. The others scan up and down.

"This Paloverle plant is unique to the Holoran Desert it does not grow anywhere else in the world. It germinates itself. It looks ruffled with eight foot branches all spread out. They should be narrowly gaped," he says.

He knocks a hoof at the base of the plant saying, "Listen to this."

Hitting three or four more times gets their attention.

Utopio says, "It sounds like a wooden hatch."

Astro finds a buried rope and all latch teeth to pull it. A huge lid below the Paloverle slides away.

"I knew it," says Spirit.

"Right! Why else would all these tracks join here? They obviously stopped here. Beastly footprints are all over the place," points Utopio.

Spirit says, "This trail was originally made by elk and cattle. Let's go in the cavern and check it out!"

"I suppose it's better to know whether or not Blaze Evil is hiding in there. What do we do if he is?" asks Astro.

Silence ensues for a moment and then Spirit gets inspired,

"Listen, studs! If any evils are in there, we will do our job and put an end to them. That is it!"

Utopio and Astro both exclaim, "Right!"

"Then let us get to it," says Spirit.

Cautiously they enter the dark lane downward.

"It is getting lighter and I hear creatures!" Astro exclaims.

Spirit replies, "Shish, lanterns below!"

"Look at these white walls!" says Topio.

He licks one and whispers, "It's salty."

The others try it as they like salt. Spirit whispers, "Sure enough it's a salt dome."

They continue exploring as the lane turns. They move past a chamber filled with white phosphorus, sulfur and sacks of arsenic. Utopio finds another chamber stacked full of platinum bars. His partners quickly gather around.

Utopio says, "Shish, listen, I hear a sloppy snort."

Slussslisshuhchahfempfah

A beast passes by without looking.

Astro moves quietly across the hall asking, "What is this?"

He sniffs a wooden door at the opening and says, "It smells like stinky sweat."

Spirit interjects saying, "Look inside at the sweet watermelons, all you could ever eat in a lifetime!"

Neatly arranged melons fill the room to the ceiling. Utopio takes his mind off food for a minute and moves into the gleaming room of precious platinum. Astro stays put dreaming about eating the watermelons. Utopio thinks of buying an enormous alfalfa field with the platinum where herds of mustangs could roam. A sign outside the property would read, "All horses may trespass!"

Spirit is astounded at their silent undaunted reactions.

Suddenly, terrible mongrels converse down the hall. The studs snap out of it and Utopio puts ears back! Guard dogs give reference to an inner stable. One beast explains he forgot to slide the lock arm shut on the gate. Just in time, he turned around and stopped the horses from escaping. The big dog thug describes pushing the gate closed with his head and pawing the latch in place.

"I kept them in, though! Thank Evil," he says.

The other beast says, "Yeah, it is lucky for you. Lucer would have had us for dinner!"

Astro whispers, "I do not think he means for company."

Topio makes the shush sign with his lips as the guards' plop their beating feet away. Astro wants to know what the stables of horses are doing here.

Spirit rightly proposes, "For laborious purposes!"

Utopio expounds on the idea saying, "For hauling everything in and out of here!"

Astro says, "We better get out while we can!"

"Not yet! We have to free those mustangs!" says Utopio.

Spirit says, "Right, we can do it. If the drool ghouls get in our way, we'll thunderbolt all over them!"

Astro concurs. He puts the plan in motion, saying, "Lead the way, chargers!"

Slipping out of the platinum chamber, they creep through the main corridor searching for the stable. A stone protruding from a wall catches their eye.

It reads, "Evil was here 3666 BC."

"Wow!" Astro responds.

"Yeah, and now he is back, but he will never return again. Come on, let's save the mustangs!" says Utopio.

He bolts leading forward.

Two black guards in a connecting hall, thump feet, making rounds. Spirit peeks around the corner and pulls his head back whispering, "Here they come!"

Astro asks, "What to do, what to do?"

The beasts enter the crossing as Utopio impersonates a stack of yellow blocks and conceals both cousins. It works. The jackals turn into another corridor not noticing anything suspicious. The way is clear. They enter the lane to the right and an eighth of a mile down another passage intersects. They turn left and find the stable only twenty-five yards ahead.

Built between opposing walls are two thick wooden doors securing wild mustangs. The doors have 32 square foot platinum frames with round platinum bars blocking the top vent. A long wooden beam braces the doors through platinum slats.

Utopio says, "Move aside boys I'll use my magic key to open this."

Placing himself in position for a perfect strike with hind legs, he pounds the beam in half. The gate door falls, *klunkity split!*

Spirit says, "Good job Topio, you are amazing. We won't worry about locking ourselves in. There it lies flat on the ground!"

Astro says, "If I knew you meant that kind of key, I could have used mine."

At the back of the large salt walled cell, seventy-six horses huddle in fear.

"It's all right. We are here to rescue," says Astro.

One mare shouts, "Look, its Utopio!"

Many mares step closer.

Utopio says, "Follow us!"

Immediately joyous whinnies ignite and a stampede rushes out into the corridor. The complex holds unfamiliar twists and turns. One hall ends, and another leads to a basin of bubbling acid.

Astro asks a mustang beside him "Is this hot pond for eliminating rebellious horses?"

The mare answers, "Oh no, it's food for the grungy beasts."

Spirit overhears and remarks, "No kidding."

He ponders flavoring their dinner with a plop of spice.

"Turn around!" Utopio distracts.

He and Spirit float up with their legs folded under their bellies above the rescued slaves leading everyone to another passage. Astro guards the rear.

Utopio signals Spirit closer and whispers in his ear, "I'll search for the exit. You keep the herd together. When I find it I'll come back for you."

He transforms into a black barn fly and travels the dark tunnel like a tiny stealth pilot. He turns left at the next junction and quickly doubles back as himself saying, "Hurry, I see sunlight."

Spirit floats above as mustangs pick up the pace following his bright tail. Utopio hears demons grumbling and motions all to stop. Ten angry guard dogs with smoking tongues enter the path in front from an adjoining hall. The steeds notice a light at the end of the tunnel. Astro flies over the herd from the rear to fight.

The dog's growl, "Grrrr-owe, grrr-uff, grrowe-uff, siss-siss-siss-er-ruff," and quickly change to "Errf, euu-ie, erruffy, owie, owe, bow-wowy, sniff, uff-uff, as put to death."

The determined pouncing hooves of Utopio, Spirit, and Astro recycle the mutts to sludge. Steam rises from the carcasses as the studs shake off pure sweat for good measure. A herd of seventy-six horses then tramples out to freedom. The last dying jackal dog beast growls, "Ruff," and fizzles out.

Far from their plight under the butte hill mesa, emancipated horses join their champions at a rendezvous in the desert. Assembled together within the walls of a dry gulch, a beaten plow horse describes his horrible experience. The rescuers sadly listen to stories of whippings, starvation, and long, hard treks in pulling heavy wagons to and from the coast. Another tells of ponies taken away aboard an incredible platinum ship.

Astro asks, "How did they catch you?"

A pinto says, "I remember how they caught me. I watched from atop the palisades. They loaded a herd onto a shiny ship. Two demons wearing capes cast twirling eye beams into my stare. Before I knew it, I had lost control. They crept into my spirit and stunned my senses. I snapped out of it when the stable doors rattled open."

Spirit requests the ships location and a buckskin stallion points' south saying, "It's at the old cattle merchants' pier. You will see holding pens and a warehouse on the beach where monsters stand guard around the clock."

Utopio explains what is happening at the spring and instructs them to go to the Regal and snowy Mountains saying, "The Indians will keep you safe on grazing land with fresh streams. Always smell water before drinking and just in case; never look an evil monster in the eyes."

The anxious mustangs absorb his guidance and depart.

Chapter 8

CAPTURE OF ASTRO

Cavanaugh's bunch follows wagon tracks across the desert to the coast. Molly shot a rattlesnake, and Hank flicked a scorpion off his boot at the last resting spot. Ben skinned the snake and rubbed the hide with rhubarb stalk to cure it. He cut the skin in half and tied the pieces around the butt of his rifle. The sections are long enough for two hatbands.

Cavanaugh cooked the meat and they ate it for lunch. Hank kept the head and rattle to scare rats out his barn. He aims to connect a spring to the mouth and rattle. It will shake at the slightest disturbance. Charlie said, 'without a preservative, the head would rot before getting home.' Hank milked the venom, hooked its fangs to a shaved prickly pear cactus leaf and dropped it into a saddlebag anyway.

An hour later across the open desert, they reach a road with many sinister powder tracks sporadically appearing over wheel ruts in both directions.

Charlie says, "Look, large monster feet stepped off a stopped wagon and I see knee prints beside this rut."

Hank says, "Look at the broken wheel on top of the century plant. They replaced it here!"

Ben says, "Three shoeless horses and a shod plow plug pulled the wagon. Look at all the tracks. I think some were mustangs."

Molly says, "They're going north with ten wide clawed dogs!"

Charlie says, "The tracks go both ways up and down the road! We will keep following to the coast!"

They lope off road over dry weeds and across arroyos. The celestial horses arrive at the Peaceful Oceans' palisades edge unnoticed behind thick brush. They witness deliveries of desolating compounds from a large platinum ship unloading full wagons of deadly cargo onto a long pier. Horrendous demons cast whips on frail pulling horses. Buckboards filled with eighty-pound arsenic bags, phosphorus blocks and sulfuric acid barrels move along the beach into a warehouse.

Adjacent to the warehouse spare horses hover in a corral waiting to load aboard the ship back to the Island of Relief. Once there, they will haul excavated composites used for increased sulfur dioxide burn-out. Slaves dump ore on conveyor belts leading it to drop into volcano throats and explode fumes out stacks. Massive yellow clouds and brimstone will fire across the ocean. Prevailing winds will send smog over bountiful Beautyland and kill all precious life.

The recon team arrives spotting something.

Charlie says, "That cactus has eyes! Ben, you sneak up closer and see what it is!"

He dismounts and moves towards it, Spirit and Astro step out from between Utopio's illusion of a century plant. Ben encourages them to follow with carrots back to the team. He returns crawling to the edge to overlook and listen. Molly, Hank and Charlie join him as Blaze Evil explains his plan to a grotesque female. It twitches the Rangers nerves. They retreat to a draw where the magical studs led their mounts for concealment and discuss it.

Charlie says, "The big costumed freak on the horse said they will return to an island. He is going to cause doom to everything. Did you hear him tell the ugly female to hurry her manasilles? I heard of them in sailor tales I thought were myths. They are primeval mutated humans called gorisilles (gor-a-silles). They can crush rocks with bare hands. We better get out of here."

Blaze under a bandit hat, leather clothes and cape, rides a big Friesian stallion shouting, "To ash with Beautyland!"

This information must reach Jake as soon as possible. Charlie knows the sea and wants to command the naval fleet to attack the platinum ship. The four Rangers cannot tackle all of the demons alone.

Molly wants to climb down the palisade and release the penned mustangs.

She mounts saying, "I have to get down there. I am going to set them free. You ride on. I'll catch up to you!"

Astro says, "Hold on I am going with you."

She darts away and Astro follows. They slide down the cliff together.

Hank shouts, "Oh no, don't do it."

He mounts kicking fast after them. The others mount and follow.

Molly and Astro reach the corral. The others stop at the ridge and watch Molly grab the gate. Astro encourages the kept horses to flee.

Blaze notices and whispers, "I see you!"

The Rangers spot him on the pier a good distance away transmitting a red pulsating beam at their eyes. The next thing you know Molly closes herself in the corral with Astro.

～∦∾

Utopio conceals the remaining team as a century plant in disbelief of what they just witnessed.

Charlie says, "Well, if that doesn't beat all? What are they trying to do?"

Spirit says, "They're hypnotized! We had better leave!"

They reluctantly gallop away to the northwest for Plentyville. Blaze suspects the captured spies were not alone.

He says to a gorisille on the dock, "We are being watched. More are out there."

The gross female says, "I have never seen a horse with a blue tail. He is a freak of nature."

Blaze once saw a horse similar to Astro and says, "Watch for a white horse with a red tail," and anxiously looks up the cliff. He boils red-faced saying, "You will catch my whip!"

His obnoxious voice travels across the desert and Utopio charges back.

Spirit shouts, "No, Topio! You will play into his hands."

Utopio stops, "I know, I know, it is not time to change the game. OK, Astro can handle this one on his own?"

Spirit says to all, "Astro has many gifts. He has neither Utopio's strength nor my wisdom, but a conquering inner music. He is capable of withstanding Blaze and protecting Molly. He will calm Evil down. Keep moving we have to get our defenses lined up. Beautyland needs protection."

Totter rump, totter rump, totter rump, totter rump go their hooves over sandy desert ground. They continue racing past small cactuses and large saguaros toward lush orchards. Thirst slows them down at a cool stream near watermelon fields.

"Take a break here. We will get to Plentyville by nightfall. Look at this burnt crop! What happened to the melons?" asks Charlie.

Spirit says, "The Evils raided, I can see their dried sludgy drools on the plants."

"Toe nail prints mark the soil in this area. It was definitely the evil's doings. This field is ruined," replies Topio.

"Dogs and man-beasts with horses and wagons were here, harvesting some and burning the rest," Spirit acknowledges.

Utopio asks Spirit, "Do you really think Astro can manage without us?"

Spirit replies, "Are you kidding me?"

Utopio rears saying, "You're right cousin! They will want to put him on a hill to pacify other slaves with song. He will be eating out of their hands like a pet. Who can resist him?"

"What about Ms. Molly though?" asks Spirit.

"I don't know?" Topio replies.

Silence ensues continuing over firm grass near a lone Elm waving cool air as they pass. Up another slope, they find carrot fields. Utopio grabs a carrot in his teeth as Spirit splits off to an apricot grove. Hank pulls a peach off a tree as he struts alongside a sparkly irrigation ditch. The other riders also find great spots to dismount and indulge the bountiful land. The horses graze in a field of Timothy grass.

Utopio and Spirit graze on thick green Bahia grass at the water's edge. Hank gives his horse to Ben and walks over to pick from a patch of maize. He gathers enough ears for everyone. Charlie goes after nearby peanuts and fills his hat to the brim. His long brown handlebar mustache shifts from side to side, as he chews. Ben goes to fill a canteen at the irrigation stream. The horses come over to take a drink when suddenly Ben shouts, "Pe-yew-ew, this water smells awful,"

He quits refilling before getting started. Everyone else drops food to run over. They recognize the garlic and rotten egg scent. The celestial steeds stay back and let the humans handle it. Spirit knows the best way to help is to let them make some discoveries on their own.

Hank shouts, "I am going to pack peaches for juice!"

Charlie and Ben agree and altogether with help from Spirit and Utopio, collect enough to last a week. The work delays the journey by about forty-minutes.

The polluted stream widens slowing them down to find a crossing. There is a narrower place upstream and they jump across. Once on the other side, they turn west up a slope and peer over the Plenty Valley. The lost time will put them there an hour or more after dark.

Ben feels heroic and kicks his horse, exclaiming, "We have to move faster! Trouble's behind and trouble's in front!"

Spirit slips into deep thought hustling over rolling hills and around alligator junipers. He catches up to Utopio and shares a wise plan. It motivates them both enough to push everyone harder to an old bridge over the river. Upon arrival, the brilliant stallions draw a map of Beaver

Lake with hooves and noses in the dirt. The men understand the construction of a dam.

Charlie rubs Utopio's neck with one hand and pets Spirit's face with the other, saying, "I have great confidence you can do it. It is worth a try."

Ben says, "Continuing without you studs is sorrowful news."

"The mission must carry on, so run boys, run with all your might!" says Hank.

Off they go, lifting into the sky, surprising everyone. The Rangers mounts nervously react in frenzy almost causing a horse wreck.

"They just lunged to the sky," says Charlie!

"Yeah watch them fly over everything! It's unbelievable," says Hank.

Spirit talks with Utopio in midair, "Your athletic form has really improved in this dimension even against gravity!"

"Indeed, and you're not doing badly yourself.

Spirit asks, "Did you know we could fly this high?"

"No, but I always wanted to. It is funny; I thought I knew our limitations but my powers work at least as well here as at home."

Spirit says, "We fly without wings. Our tails and manes work aerodynamically enough to do anything in this air."

The men watch them gliding for a while before crossing the wooden overpass.

Hank asks, "What other magic do they possess?"

Ben says, "I don't know."

Charlie goes across saying, "Those studs are going to be a great help! Now remount and move on!"

Spirit discusses the fate of Astro and Molly with Utopio.

"Astro is on the way to Relief Island. We need to fly faster!"

"Right, I am propelling with a mighty ambition. I trust he can handle things on his own for a while."

"No worries cousin!"

They continue side by side up river into pristine beaver country north of the spring.

Chapter 9

DETERMINATION

While flying along Utopio explains his under-standing of the plan, "Let me get this straight. The bucktoothed beavers will block the river and create a lake?"

Spirit says, "Yes, that is it! The river bottom will dry out, and the poisonous residue will wash away at the right time."

Topio asks, "What if the beasts discover the dam?"

Spirit thinks for a minute and answers, "We will create a larger hidden reservoir below the spring. It will become the Army's new arsenal and hold enough drinking water for everyone."

Utopio says, "The trick is to keep it fresh and out of sight. Afterwards, we'll destroy their poisonous supply at the caverns!"

Spirit answers, "Right, 'who can be against us when God is with us'?"

Utopio adds "We had to stay invisible and on the ground against the Gejacom warriors in the last Great War. Strong Am, our master, left most means of victory up to Jake. This time our visibility is at our own discretion. We can be seen if we want to, and not seen when we don't. The only three dimensions others see here are of no comparison to our powers. We can fly and so much more. This war is our duty to end.

Spirit reiterates, "The Gejacom's invasion used simple manpower not like this devil. I guess this time Strong Am wants to let the demons know who they are up against."

Utopio says, "I wish Astro was here. He would say something like, "The mighty steeds are we three." Let not your hearts, troubled be!"

"Our power is greatly equipped with eternal life," says Spirit.

"Those who would harm Beautyland will feel God's 'strong arm through us for sure," says Utopio.

"Evil's reign must end in this just war. The Beaulancians did not cause his envy. Our power continues to grow. I can feel it," says Spirit.

Utopio acknowledges, "Strong Am, the God of God's, created this land to thrive. It is the paradise for loving followers. The more damage inflicted, then the, stronger we fight for rights. Beaulancians must avoid the enemy. I will divert the spring under the riverbed and drill a waterway to the lone elm. The first length will be twenty-feet in diameter and run deep under the river. Every ten thousand yards, I will decrease the diameter by two feet. The shrinking size will pressurize the flow and quickly fill the basin at the arroyo. I will build temporary Beaulancian homes under the whole territory. They will have plenty of comfort and water enough to last long after the intrusion!"

Sprit says, "Beaver Lake is just ahead! Take off now to do your digging and I will finish the dam alone."

Utopio says, "You be the brains and I'll be the brawn."

During the last twenty-four hours, Jake and Will retrieved water from a high glacier stream. They followed an elk trail cutting down the mountain to within fifteen miles of town. Approaching Plentyville, Jake says, "Do not to speak to anyone about the invasion until absolutely necessary. We have no time to deal with frenzy in the streets. This is Sunday and the Chief will be indisposed. We will see him tomorrow at the Presidential Mansion."

Everything downtown looks normal. It is eight thirty in the morning as they approach the, "Plenty Good Corral." Quintin Smith, the owner and town's best blacksmith, greets them saying, "You are lucky men. Thirty minutes earlier, I sold a prized black-and-white Appaloosa to some strange, foreign fella. I do have two empty stalls. I tell you what; I'll let you have each for two bits a day!"

They agree but have difficulty in negotiating an early pickup. Quintin says, "The platinum bar I took in is worth thirty ponies just like it. I's feeling rich and I's going to celebrate! Yes, sirs, I's gonna celebrate late tonight and sleep long in the morning! If 'in ya needs 'em back before 5:30 a.m., justa pay me .50 cents in advance. I's will groom and shod's 'em for ya's today. Youse fellas cans picks 'em up any time you want tomorrow whether I's here or not!"

His spit tobacco twangs on an old metal milk canister. He says, "Take a gander at dis heavy molded platinum bar fellas. It is so shiny. The red and black haired stranger said, 'It won't never tarnish.' Yes *sirree*, it is a valuable stake for retirement! I'm a going to put it away somewhere safe. Give me a minute."

Jake asks, "Say, just a second smithy, did the buyer mention how he came upon that bar or say where he himself came from?"

Quintin begrudges the question saying, "I's doesn't never look a gift buyer in the pocket. Besides, he said ifin I could round up twenty more horses, he'd give me twenty more bars!"

Will asks, "What the blazes did he want with all of those horses and why is he willing to pay such a high price?"

Quintin explains, "Like I says, I's doesn't ask questions of a good customer. He paid and I's told's him I's didn't have no change. He doesn't care, so I's doesn't care. I's rich and I's going to get richer and that's all's I's knows!"

I told him there ain't no horse worth that much but he says he aint's got nothin' smaller and the bars only weigh him down anyhow! I's doesn't knows how's come he's wastin' so much on a pachamaimy horse.

I's just glad's, he is. I's gots his name down on a receipt, ifin you're so interested, looky here!"

It reads as follows:

Date sold: March 9 1877
One spotted black on white six-year Appaloosa stallion.
Name: Storm Cloud!
Sold to: Cain Evilson.
Received: Two-pound platinum bar.
Paid In Full.

This occurrence plays out in Jake's mind all throughout the day. They check into the Harmony Hotel, only a half-mile walk from the stables. The wide dirt Main Street divides shops on both sides. Boardwalks connect small wooden storefronts. Their hotel is between a restaurant and a barbershop. It is caddy corner to the Tipsy Maker Saloon. Carriages and horse riding traffic is always slight on Sunday mornings.

The hotel sign advertises a bathhouse, and the men want to go directly to it after checking in. They book a room upstairs with double beds. Jake sees a restaurant across the street out the window. The, "Plenty Good Café," advertises home-style meals and describes beef tips, green beans, yellow buttered squash, corn bread, and apple pie."

Jake asks, "Are you hungry?"

"Man, I am," says Will.

They clean up using two full water basins on the dresser next to fresh towels and skip the bath to go out for vittles right now. The only choices available on the menu this morning include bacon, eggs and all the flapjacks they can eat for .35cents per person. Church bells ring while slopping down the feed. These are hungry men but they finish quickly and walk over to it.

Upon entering the sermon giver asks, "Who can be against you if God is with you?"

Jake nudges Will to stay standing in the back and whispers, "This is my new favorite sermon."

Will asks, "What was your old one?"

Jake whispers, "Blessed are the peacemakers," as he bows his head.

They return to the hotel after service and fall fast asleep. Goodman's mind twirls with Cain's slight description fading in and out. In a dream, he realizes the wealthy horseman could be a descendant of the notorious Blaze Evil and the suspicion is startling.

He says, "Will, wake up! There is no time to dillydally."

In search of more clues, they question the front desk clerk and pedestrians within two square miles. Finally, a boy about ten years of age, found sitting in a tree at a park behind the hotel tells them of an incident from earlier this morning.

He says, "I went to the general store to buy some candy but it was closed. So on way to my friend's house I saw some huge hairy manlike creatures with red eyes waiting on a buckboard."

Wills asks, "Red eyes?"

"Yes sir, red eyes! One held the reins to two lathered horses and two sat on the back eating yellow blocks. Then a man with long black-and-red hair rode up on a black and white Appaloosa with four mean dogs running alongside. I hid in this tree. They were vicious mister. I ain't never seen meaner such dogs in my whole life. They had green fangs as long as my pinky. One creature threw a block and them dogs commenced to fighting over it. The horseman made 'em stop with a whip. I was so scared I closed my eyes. I heard them go away. I didn't want to come down. I fell asleep. Do you think it was all a dream, mister? I never saw them again."

Jake says, "Maybe it was son!"

Will says, "These creatures might be the same we tracked from the farmhouse yesterday. I wonder what happened to the family."

Jake asks the boy, "What is your name, son?"

"Chester," he says.

Jake asks, "Chester, did you see any folks with them?"

"No, sir!" he says.

Will asks, "Is there anything more you can remember?"

He pauses and says, "I remember a bundle of rope sittin' atop a stack of them blocks in the buckboard."

Jake thinks, *Rope, to pull the abducted family.*

Things were adding up. He presses Chester once more asking, "Where did they go?"

The youngster explains, "I never seen 'em leave, sir! My eyes closed. I could not stand another look. I didn't want to follow after them neither sir! You might look behind the grain silo. The sound seemed to go that way!

Jake asks, "Otherwise, it was a regular quiet Sunday, huh, son?"

Chester says, "Yes sir!"

The men leave to search past the silo until late afternoon. The trail leads nowhere. They return to the hotel for more shut-eye and in the morning, will present everything to the President.

Chapter 10

ENSLAVED

Cavanaugh's company draws near the edge of town catching a glimpse of freakish Cain Evil, the son of Blaze. He rides the Appaloosa leading an overloaded buckboard and four crony dogs along a road through meadowland. Immediately, Charlie, Hank, and Ben take cover behind red maple trees and watch through spyglasses. The aliens drift off road through a grassy field toward a wagon manufacturing plant. The sun is setting as double front doors open. They glimpse bound people sitting on the floor against a wall. The odd creatures enter and the doors shut.

Charlie says, "I saw some forty people with wrists tied to a two-inch tow line."

"Look past the building to the top of the hill. See the sentries?" asks Hank.

"I do and two more climbing to the top. I suppose it is the next shift coming on. We will go to the woods behind the warehouse, sneak up the hill and snatch them for interrogation," Charlie instructs.

Ben asks, "Do you really think we can do it? Them are monstrous boys, ya know?"

Charlie looks through the scope again and replies, "Ben, I heard tell you once lassoed a bear and tied up all four limbs singlehandedly. I heard you dragged it from the mountains on a handmade travois. They say you traveled all the way to the city and won the bear-wrestling contest. In fact, aren't you riding the prize pony right now?"

He replies, "Yep, this is Sugarfoot!"

Charlie says, "You and Hank are at your best in dangerous situations. What are you afraid of, a few hairy rascals? Come on!"

"Wait, we can do this. I have an idea," says Ben.

They unwind ropes attached to saddle horns and prepare lassoes.

"We will come roping from behind and wrap 'em together in our tarps," he adds.

Charlie says, "Good plan but carefully or the tarps could tear!"

"There's a bluff with caves on the other side of the hill. Let's take them there!" Hank suggests.

"Yeah, good idea," says Ben.

"All right, let's make it happen!" says Charlie.

They cut in and out of trees in the woods to the highest point behind the guards and peek around boulders over the lookout hill. Two lone furry sentries wearing black dog-skin overalls wave "all is well" to the two they replaced from the last shift reentering the factory's back door and Charlie whispers, "It's all clear, wait for my signal and rope like there's no tomorrow!"

The new gorisille sentries each pick up boulders for sitting and watch the sunset. South beyond the city, clouds form over the Peaceful Ocean. Southeastern orchards cover thousands of acres. A Pecan treetop rests below their hanging feet and to the right is a jagged red cliff across Faiths Creek. Behind them lies ten miles of rugged woods forming the northern foothills. The road from the city is their main concern with traveler exposure concealed under a corridor of elm, maple and willow branches. Their eyesight and hearing is bad and night vision is worse. What looks like a storm brewing over the ocean distracts attention. These two rather short gorisilles sit lazily with long black furry, bare arm and shoulder hairs, waving in wind.

The rushing creek obscures sounds and the soft hilltop grass encourages quiet hooves on attack.

"Are you ready?" Charlie asks.

Hank says, "Let's get it done."

"I'm ready!" says Ben.

"Ready, set, go!" Charlie says leading onward.

Ben's rope lands one. Hank snags the other and Charlie throws a loop over both. They reel in tightly as the horses turn around close enough to kick them over the cliff. The beast's growl but the men dismount and cover head to toe with tarps. Hank wraps twine down to their feet. One beast bites through the canvas drooling red-hot vomit on Hank's glove. It burns clean through. He grits teeth trying not to shout, "Owe" and shakes it off finishing the knot with an aching hand.

Charlie wraps tight twine around their heads and jaws to shut them up. Ben ties an extra tarp over their heads. They remount and swat horses down a goat trail dragging the bundle to the creek. Hank's horse stumbles and slides. Ben blocks it from rolling to regain footing as Charlie warns, "Hang on!"

Hanks' wounded hand hurts. He plans to see a doctor as soon as possible. At the side of the creek, Ben smells something awful in the water and holds his nose. The others smell it too. Ben's horse lowers its head, sucks up a drink and falls over within seconds. Ben jumps off to the edge of shore holding the rope. The horse jerks in a thrust to stand but falls completely into the stream and dies drifting away.

Ben cries, "Yikes!"

Charlie sees barrels, sacks and yellow blocks, sticking out on a ledge across the creek. He asks, "Is everyone all right?"

They affirm and he says, "They have chemical compounds on the other side."

Hank says, "There may be more gorisilles!"

Ben mounts behind Hank.

Hank asks, "How do we get over there?"

Charlie asks Hank, "Can you swim?"

He answers, "Yes! What about you?"

Charlie nods yes, saying, "Wade across! I'll throw you a rope."

He hands his end of the tug line to Charlie and dismounts to step into the stream with tightly shut lips. His head goes under in a crashing billow. Ben takes hold of a root in the water and reaches out an arm. Hank grabs on and Ben pulls him out.

"Woo! That was close the current is strong! I got washed but I don't smell any better!" Hank jokes.

Charlie says, "Let's try it again and be quiet!"

Hank takes another rope off his saddle, ties a rock and throws it over a downed tree on the other side. It settles and the three men hoist the demons over the back of Charlie's horse.

"Ben, hang on to the line and wade out to the first big rock and rap some slack once around. Make sure it holds. OK you did it, very well. Keep going and wrap another bit around the next one and pull yourself out. Tie the other end down good on that tree," says Charlie.

He ties his end to a nearby tree saying, "Hank hold the line, walk your horse across and I'll follow."

Out in the middle of the crossing, Hank asks, "How are the gorisilles doing? Don't let 'em drown!"

"They're riding high and dry!" Charlie exclaims.

Once across, they climb up a path built into the jagged cliff to a cave large enough for horses. They feel safe inside and discuss the disappearance of Ben's mount.

Charlie brings forth a first-aid tin and applies clean water and salve to Hanks hand. The burn is deep and he will surely scar.

Ben asks, "Does it feel any better yet?"

Hank says, "Yeah, it does but I sure could use a good swig of whiskey about now!"

"Just hold on old buddy. You can celebrate when we're all done," Charlie says and unties the tarps.

Hank replies, "Be careful!"

Charlie says, "Don't worry. I am not going to take all the ropes off. You two hold their foreheads to the ground with your boots. I'll cut the jaw strings and we can get them talking."

Ben replies, "You bet!"

"I'm ready!" shouts Hank.

Charlie slices the twine with a long skinner knife and removes the tarps.

Both creatures raise eyelids above purple crystalline peepholes casting red translucent beams to Charlie's eyes. They overpower and encourage him to stab Hank and Ben. He grabs a knife from a boot and with glassy eyes raises the blade. He looks crazed and charges but stops midway. He contorts and falls unconscious to the dirt.

Hank shouts, "Charlie, what are you doing?"

Ben is flabbergasted and looks to the demons.

He points, saying, "Freshwater is dripping down from the ceiling and look, they're dead!"

"The drops put out the beasts, look they're smoldering," Hank acknowledges.

Charlie shakes his head, snaps out of it, and gets up.

"Are you all right?" Hank asks.

Charlie answers, "Yeah, why, what happened?"

"Look up, see those drips? They killed 'em!" Hank agrees.

"They really did kill 'em. I saw it and look now they're just a pile of fur," notices Ben.

Charlie asks, "What happened to me?"

Hank explains, "Their eyes lit up and shot beams at you. All of a sudden you acted really scary and tried to stab us!"

Bens adds, "That's for sure. You clenched your knife in the air, and came at us like we're the enemy. You were going to kill us. I didn't know what I to do and then you collapsed."

Hank asks, "Are you sure you have back your wits yet, Charlie?"

"Of course I do," he answers.

Ben asks, "Ah, would you mind putting that knife away, then?"

"Oh, sure, yeah, my knife," and he sticks it back into the sheath inside a boot.

Hank wonders, "OK, that's over, now what?"

Charlie stares at the ashes of the two demons saying, "Strange way to die. Little drips of water put two big droolers down, drips for bigger drips, hmm! Fill your canteens and lets' get to Plentyville. We can rent a couple of rooms and in the morning find Jake."

Hank insists, "Yeah, recoil the ropes, pack up and let's go."

Ben agrees, "We're out of here!"

The stream narrows closer to town and Ben happily finds his horse washed up over rocks on the other side. They wade across and retrieve Ben's tack and hoists it over the loins of Charlie's gelding. Ben hops up behind Hank and they ride alongside the turning creek under trees in darkness. Further, on down, the tree cover lessens exposing meadows before city streets. They gallop to hurry away from openness.

The only noise downtown is theirs on this early Sunday night. Quaint stone homes line the road and Charlie recognizes one. He remembers a road intersecting up ahead will take them to the hotel.

He instructs, "We turn left in a block or two more. We went a little too far past Fifth Street. Two blocks down is Main Street. We turn left, go to the end and turn left once more to the hotel. From there only a mile away is the Plenty Good Stables."

Twenty-five minutes later, they find the hotel and register. They ride to the closed stables and secure the horses themselves. Charlie leaves a note saying he will come in the morning to pay. They walk back to the hotel hungry but the downtown restaurants are closed. Early tomorrow becomes chow time at an uptown café. They will then go to the stables and purchase a new mount. After business, it is on to the President's Mansion. Hank and Ben share a room wrestling within sheets fighting today's tragic memories. They pray for Molly, Astro, and all the good people held in the wagon factory. Hank's hand hurts.

"Sleep," he keeps telling himself, "sleep!"

Ben is snoring as light breaks through the thin window curtain. Hank rises relieved the night is over. He dips a washcloth in large bowl thinking about the incident at the cavern again. He wakes Ben, telling him to hurry and goes across the hall, to wake Charlie but notices the door wide open. He goes downstairs to check the lobby and hears Charlie's voice at the front desk. His broad six-foot-three-inch frame overshadows the clerk. Ben rushes to the desk and the nervous clerk asks, "How was your rest, gentlemen?"

"Not good!" the brawny men all answer.

Hank says, "But by no fault of the hotel, sir."

That is all they say at check out for fear of frightening him anymore. Outside on the wooden front porch, Charlie looks over all their dirty clothes and says, "I hope the café will serve us."

Hank's thoughts conclude and he says, "Fellas, I don't think these gun belts are going to help much against this enemy. I am going up the street to the wine merchant. I have an idea about wineskins."

Ben interrupts saying, "Last night, I was thinking about water weapons. They could fit our sides. We could attach better nozzles to improve distance."

"Great minds think alike, huh men. Do you think they could pump at least fifty feet?" asks Charlie.

Hank replies, "You never know until you try. What do you think? It's worth a try isn't it?"

"Water killed those devils with only a few drops. Let's do it," says Ben.

Charlie knocks dirt off his Patriot hat against a leg and skips breakfast to get it done.

Hank stops walking, saying, "The largest ones hold three gallons. That should last a long time. It only takes a few drips to kill 'em. We could get plenty of shots off."

Charlie asks, "You're a good leather man, aren't you, Hank?"

"I could make better fitting shoulder and waste straps," he says.

"Pumping underarm should easily bellow powerful streams. Lets' make the squirts hurt," says Ben.

Hank replies, "It's definitely worth a try."

"OK! How about we eat first and then see the wine merchant. What do you say, men? I am hungry. How 'bout it, you're hungry, right?" asks Charlie.

Hank replies, "I am and it sounds good to me."

Ben agrees, "OK! The skins are going to cost though. How much money do you boys hold?"

"Don't worry; I sold twelve cows before we hit the trail and brought most the proceeds with me. We'll be good for a while," Charlie remarks.

"You're gonna have to take me to a doctor. My hand needs looking at and I ain't got much money on me," Hank complains.

"We will get that hand looked at first thing after breakfast," suggests Ben.

Charlie concurs, "Indeed we will! The doc is not open yet. Let's eat."

"I have enough to share. Don't worry about money at a time like this Hank. We are all in this together," adds Ben.

Charlie agrees, "We'll do just fine."

The men eat and walk to a doctor's office. He suggests the hand will mend in two weeks. The scar will boldly show for five years. He puts on salve, wraps it with bandage and offers a swig of codeine for the pain.

Hank replies, "It really don't hurt so much anymore with the salve on it, Doc!"

The doctor hands the codeine to him anyway and more to Ben with a complete medical kit for the trail.

At the stables, Ben acquires a winsome buckskin gelding after haggling forty-five minutes with a fill in for Smith. The physically Herculean new assistant, Jimmy O'Dye Mills, was unwilling to settle for less than thirty dollars. The horse is worth it and Ben pays all the boarding fees besides. Charlie and Hank now deal to trade in their horses. Charlie pays another sixty dollars for two more geldings, a bay for Hank and a sorrel for himself. He adds a tip. The horses are newly shod and ready to go. Jimmy lifts his eyebrows as high as his curly black bangs smiling and staring at his two handfuls of money saying, "I love this job!"

He shakes hands with massive fingers and helps them mount.

Charlie says, "Goodbye O'Dye Mills!"

"Yes sir, it's a pleasure, you's can call me Jimmy. Come again and be sure to see me! I'll do you right!"

"We will, Jimmy," Ben agrees.

"Thank you Charlie! This horse has a good gate," Hank remarks.

Three blocks away, the wine merchant provides skins. Ben samples one. He blasts a flowerpot hanging from a second-story balcony across the street and hollers, "Yeah, doggie herders, this will get ya!"

Charlie asks the proprietor, "How many do you have?"

He counts inventory answering, "Fifteen!"

Charlie takes all and to Hank, explains,

"They hold ample water. Give the shoulder straps a better fit. We can pick up some brass nozzles at the hardware store."

Hank adds, "They need more range."

Ben adds, "Fine, but how mine already shoots is not half bad. What are we going do with so many? They'll be awful heavy when filled."

"Reinforcements, to supply Jake and Will and for spares," Charlie assures.

"A fight in the desert needs plenty of water. You can bet on that," Hank insists.

Charlie agrees, "We're prepared!"

"You bet," says Ben.

Charlie adds, "Each horse can carry five. One hundred twenty five extra pounds won't hurt on the short ride to The Mansion. We're all lightweights with room to spare."

The storekeeper charges fifty dollars. Charlie pays and they attach the equipment to their mounts. The seller watches from the front stoop and asks, "What you aim to do with those wineskins? Going to have one heck of a party, are ya?"

Hank answers "Right!"

"We are gonna make shooters," says Ben.

The storekeeper removes his glasses and watches their dust as they race to the hardware store. Once there, Hank rigs on better nozzles. They move on to the leather shop for waste straps. The wineskins now squeeze streams up to a hundred feet and stay sturdy on their sides. They meander through the streets among other shoppers in the late

morning until reaching The President's Mansion. Tall iron fencing sur-
rounds it and guards at the main gate adhere to strict security measures.
The office will not open for visitors until 11:00 a.m.

Chapter 11

MESSAGE TO THE HOUSE

Charlie seeks information about Jake's whereabouts from the Mansions guards. They maintain no one else has arrived and a meeting with the President requires leaving all weapons at the Plenty Good Stables and Livery.

"Here we go again," says Ben.

They quickly return and Charlie sees Jake and Will leading their horses out of the barn. He dismounts saying, "Lo and behold look who's here!"

Jake greets Charlie with a tight hug saying, "I am so glad to see you. What is the enemy up to?"

Hank answers, "Plenty!"

Will notices his soggy bandaged hand and asks, "What trouble did you get into?"

Jake prevents the answer on the spot to keep the stable hands from hearing. He suggests more privacy at a large oak thirty yards behind the barn. Once there, Charlie explains in detail. Jake and Will are relieved to learn the families are only captive and still alive. Jake gives account of his exploits and they all have a good laugh for recognizing the same use of weaponry.

Jake says, "Great minds think alike!"

Charlie asks, "What's our next move, Jake?"

"It's time to tell the President!" He exclaims.

"How are we going to explain it?" asks Ben.

Jake thinks for a moment and suggests Ben, Will, and Hank stay behind.

He says, "Wait up the street in the café until Charlie and I return. It would be best not to overwhelm the President. We can give the full account alone without scaring him to death. The delivery is crucial and it will take some time! All in agreement, say, Aye?"

They all answer, "Nay!"

Jake replies, "All right, we will do this together. That's what I like, team spirit, so let's get to it!"

They drop off their weapons with Mills and trot back to the Mansion. One guard frisks them at the gate and two others tie up their horses. A coachman takes them along a winding drive past manicured lawns and lush gardens to the front door.

President Solomon F. Dulcet himself meets them at the front door between two sentries saying, "Good morning, gentlemen, this must be some matter of great importance you look a bit less for wear."

Jake says, "It concerns all of Beautyland, sir!"

"Yes, sir, it does directly, Mr. President," says Charlie.

Dulcet replies "Well then come in and talk to me!"

Once all are in two other guards secure the heavy door from the inside. Dulcet leads them to his finely furnished soundproof office. He sits on a top-grade blue satin seat. His mahogany chair with gold inlays sets behind a marble-top mahogany desk. The room features many ornate paintings on the walls. However, nothing captures their attention quite like the tall wood and enamel painted rearing horse to the right of the entrance facing the fireplace. The mare's white body has red enamel bands running down its back to the tail dock. They fork at the loins and divert down hind legs to black tiptoed hooves. The white ears each with red dividing lines point at the entrance behind its rearing head. Double half-inch lines run down the forehead. Single red circles surround blue eyes. Two one-inch wide vertical breast bands split down rearing front legs to black hooves. The mane and tail flow red and white.

Ben cannot take his eyes off this amazingly realistic work of art and touches the bottom lip asking, "Where did you get this magnificent carving?"

The President answers, "It was here when I took over. I never look a gift horse in the mouth, hahaha!"

Jake and Charlie sit in blue chairs in front of the desk. Will, Hank, and Ben sit on a premium red leather sofa facing their backs. The fireplace behind them is alive regardless of the pleasant weather and the room is very warm. The mantel holds bronze statuettes of King Harmonious and an eagle. Small portraits of past Presidents border the walls. Ceiling sections have painted accents of Beautyland with a beautiful crystal chandelier hanging down from the center. Blue, red, gold, and white drapes fit a bay window at the far end of the room. Bookshelves align the wall to the left of the President's desk. Two additional little sitting areas decorate the remainder of the office.

Dulcet watches the speechless men notice the ornately decorated room and asks Jake,

"Haven't I seen you somewhere before? Maybe it was when I was Governor of Apple Valley? No, no of course, I know who you are. You're the courageous General Goodman who led us to victory in the last war. Forgive me; I did not immediately recognize you, sir! What emergency brings you to me, aren't you enjoying retirement General?"

Jake says, "Yes, well I was sir, but Mr. President, another very turbulent time is upon us!"

Charlie says, "That is why we are all here, Mr. President!"

"You must be Captain Cavanaugh, another great hero, might I have known? Well sir, will this involve the Navy?" He asks.

Charlie says, "Indeed, Mr. President, there is a great threat requiring all forces, sir."

"Of course a threat, what is this threat?" asks President Dulcet.

Jake stands removing his Patriot hat and slides fingers over a thick dark mustache. He moves to the edge of the sofa next to Ben and Will as he considers how to answer that. Hank feels a bit queasy from codeine and stands resting an elbow quietly on a hoof of the rearing horse sculpture.

Jake gives a simple explanation, "Hordes of demons under the command of a black caped mad man named Blaze have invaded Beauty with chemical weaponry!"

The President's heart pounds in reply, "After so many centuries how could this be? I thought he was only a fable!"

The President postpones all other business. Four hours pass in discussion and finally he says, "Something told me when I awoke this morning and had to swat a fly off the First Lady, it was going to be a bad day. I had no idea it would be this bad!"

Charlie says, "Nothing like this ever crossed my mind before either, sir. I could hardly believe my ears when Jake's son told me."

"It is all true, sir! It is what it is! We have all seen with our own eyes. It is up to you now, sir," Jake adds.

The 5'8", gray headed and slightly balding pudgy man sits pounding a teletype to all branches of the armed forces saying,

"Prepare battle stations. We are under attack."

He glances up at the waiting Rangers saying, "I don't know how we can fight this enemy with water. Our forces are not equipped to maneuver tons and tons of water to each battle. Moreover, Gentlemen do you really believe water skins alone will kill all these demons. I don't know about this."

"Well, sir, that's the situation. It is what it is. We know you will want to think on it. Give us an accompaniment of two platoon sections to assist in freeing the captives and we will get on it right away," Jake insists.

Dulcet says, "Yes, of course, right away!"

He types a dispatch to send twelve soldiers to meet Jake at the Plenty Good Corral and the bearers of bad news say farewell.

The President asks, "When will I hear from you again?"

Jake answers from already out the front door, "We'll send reports whenever possible, Mr. President."

The Rangers mosey over to the, "Plenty Good Café," with time to kill. The fort is twenty miles away. They manage waiting having fun with the pretty server as the day looms on.

Chapter 12

HOSTAGE RESCUE

Cain awakes this morning in the back of a wagon to unsettling findings. His dawn shift sentries discover the night shift is missing and hoof prints give away the details. They tracked to the cave and found gorisille remains and the horse carcass. The sentries returned to the plant gurgling and screeching through gapped teeth. Cain realizes his whereabouts is now threatened. Red lights strobe on walls inside the building from demonic gorisille eyes. Cain's red ears flap and his green tongue lashes out corrosive feminine sounding voice inflections. Twenty-three employees and the owner of the factory sit among other captives in fear. Nine men including the owner and two women have families at home thinking they are working overtime.

While raised by female concubines, Cain learned to connive in a very un-manlike manner. Some of the prisoners have not had a substantial meal in over a week. Thank goodness for little children. They like to carry apples, pecans, walnuts, peanuts, and candy in their pockets. These mostly farm boys had combined enough food to share plenty of fragments until yesterday. Today the fifty or so hostages may go hungry again.

The demons will sure enough release their bindings for work even earlier today without offering any food. The strongest ones build buckboards and the weaker ones stay seated and tied to the thick towline.

Cain says, "I want knowledge. Who can tell me who was here last night? The first to say will be fed and if it is the correct answer I will feed everyone."

No one knows to answer. He laughs giving them a break from beatings with confidence anyway saying, "I need my hair fixed."

A demon unties a pretty woman to arrange his hair in a more dignified style. Cain shouts, "Bring me two children."

A burly demon unleashes two and presents them to him on the wagon bench. He entertains himself sadistically tickling the kids with long sharp fingernails. They push deeper as he thinks over last night's occurrence. Suddenly, he drops the kids and stands, shouting, "None will escape. Be useful or die!"

He releases them to gather cronies for a meeting in preparation for an assumptive attack on the warehouse. He has all the people gagged with bandanas and stands them on scaffolds in front of the windows looking out.

～٨ﾍ～

Meanwhile, blacksmith Quintin works diligently hammering new horseshoes on an old nag. The Rangers spent all night at the café in waiting for the cavalry thanks to the server. They leave for the stables after a big breakfast. Jake rides ahead to arriving soldiers and discreetly says to a Lieutenant, "We are after very treacherous creatures and issuing you the weapons of choice. Fill 'em up at the water pump. These skins will do the trick.

The Lieutenant says, "Really, what happens if we only use our carbines sir?"

"Then you end up as doggie fodder, Lieutenant. You will not need rifles or pistols. They won't kill these beasts," Jake insists.

The Lieutenant says under his breath, "I might hold on to my guns just in case."

Charlie distributes twelve wineskins and the soldiers form a line at the pump. After filling, they move out in formation on the forty-minute trail to the wagon plant.

President Dulcet sends a wire to Fort Intrepid ordering Special Forces to inspect the River running through the city. During this time, Hank scouts off road ahead of the other sixteen-men. He stands behind a wide Oak using a spyglass to peer around the grounds and sees the captives at windows. The demons are nowhere in sight so he leaps back on his horse and swiftly moves forward. The meadow dips into a draw allowing concealment. He maneuvers across to a grove near the rear of the factory.

He sneaks between trees around a corral holding captured mustangs and plow plugs. His horse steps quietly up a slope to thicker woods as a gruff sounding dog barks inside the building. Slower sounds resonate to the outside in sentences unable to interpret. The spyglass reveals more muzzled people looking out the rear windows. Cain's two-toned hair occasionally passes between their spaces. The back door opens and he steps out with five demons and six dogs to the top of the lookout post.

Hank wonders how to get the information back unscathed. Cain could see the cavalry coming from the hill. Twelve other monsters step outside and split up around the building. Hank guesses nearly a hundred captives inside. He has to inform the others quickly. Two more thugs step out, look around and close the door, from the inside. Hank then quietly leads his horse by the reins down a wooded slope to a gully and remounts in the lowest place. He trots up and across the road to reach the section safely from the far side. He reports under a canopy of Elms.

Jake formulates a plan saying, "I will take four soldiers to the front and draw attention. Lieutenant, you take two plus Hank and charge the back door. Ben and four others will hunt the demons outside the compound. Charlie, you ride with Will and another soldier past the hill to the creek. Catch anything trying to sneak away. Has everyone got it?"

"Yes, sir," they all confirm.

Jake says, "Form your parties!"

Teams separate.

Jake asks, "Ready?"

They all respond, "Ready, sir!"

Jake raises an arm and thrusts it down quickly shouting, "Move out!"

Ben's team charges first. Spanish moss spookily hangs from oaks on the grounds before the factory. Three demons lying in tall grass jump off their bellies roaring in front of the horses and cause a ruckus. Ben blasts two dead. A soldier kills another. They place hobbles on the horse's front legs behind a big oak and spread out on stomachs searching for more.

~∿~

Jake's team cautiously rides up to the main entrance unscathed. The Lieutenant's team with Hank makes it to the woods behind the back and waits for action. Charlie, Will, and a soldier stick close to ground cover and move around Ben to the creek. The one wide wooden front door is chain locked. Jake catches a glimpse of a beast looking at them atop the adjacent hill. He pulls his sidearm and blasts the lock apart. Hostages watch with gagged mouths in amazement through the upper windows. Jake readies the water skin from underarm. He pulls the reins hard back and with a swift kick at the same time forces his horse to rear. The hooves crash down breaking the latch. The door swings open and they storm in.

Beasts waiting in the rafters jump down at Jakes whole team. They can only fearfully watch as the evil ones cast rays into their eyes from wicked electric staffs. The raiders freeze in position like manikins but their horses are unaffected. The Lieutenant and a Corporal enter through the back door catching rays. The horses are so afraid they stand shivering in fear with nowhere to run in the crowded warehouse. The beasts hold them in place and the riders are speechless. Hank with another soldier witnesses this through the back doorway in time to skedaddle away. He finds Cain's pointed boot tracks and two demon prints leading around the north side of the hill, across the creek, into the foothills.

Meanwhile, Ben with four-soldiers finds a lone demon sleeping near the creek beside a split boulder.

Ben says, "Look at this, Corporal!"

The Corporal says, "His head is swollen like a melon. Look at the rocky part of the hill. I can see where a chunk broke off. He is unconscious!"

Ben says, "Right, bind him up. The little devil could come in handy if he can talk."

The Corporal reaches for a bedroll behind the saddle cantle saying, "After I's throws this tarp on him you men help lifts him to the horse, best be protectin 'yourn' ownselves now! Dis critter is hot, and I's doesn't wants to git burned ta."

Ben says, "We ought to find Charlie downstream along the creek."

A Private says, "Look, tracks!"

The Corporal shouts, "Horses crossed the creek just minutes ago, sir!"

Ben adds, "Dogs and beasts followed them and stopped at the edge. Look across the creek. I can see Charlie's team. They are going into the cave. Come on!"

They race across with the prisoner bouncing on the loins of the Corporal's horse. Tracks lead around a bend and up muddy rocks to the cave. They hide behind a bulging crag at the bend. Six jackals guard the entrance. A raging wall of fire blocks the opening. Another Private dismounts and climbs the jagged rock to see behind the flames.

He whispers, "I can see Charlie, Will and another soldier, tied and trapped. They look all right but they aren't moving."

In a second look, he realizes they are sitting on motionless horses and makes his way back down. He remounts, saying to Ben,

"Sir, every man and horse alike stands as still as rocks, and three demons on the ground play dice."

They trek back to catch Jake, thinking the rescue is over and stop short at a large Pecan grove four hundred yards before the building.

Bens says, "It is an awful quiet battle. Is everyone inside all right? The hostages still look out the windows. It is a literal standstill!"

Suddenly, eleven demons jump out from behind bushes beaming staff rays without a tussle. They stun two soldiers. Big Ben jumps off his horse and wrestles a small one to the ground to keep it from ripping the bit out of the horse's mouth. He twists the nozzle and pumps it dead between the eyes. He takes its staff and packs it away. He turns around quickly and kills four more. One of the last soldiers' fires streams at three demons and puts those down. Another monster uses the horses of the stunned mounted soldiers as cover and beams the other soldier. Now he sits on his horse frowning with dazzled eyes. Ben ducks until finally beams catch him too. The horses keep still, only shivering, with too much fear to move and the trap is complete.

A big beastly demon unravels the unconscious demon on the Corporal's horse and tosses him to the ground. The intended informant awakes spitting fuming red lava and grumbling accusations. Three other beasts grab reins and lead the dazed horsemen into the building to join the others. All of the reunited rescuers are speechlessly hypnotized. This accounts for everyone but Hank and a Private. Cain and two other demons still wander around somewhere in the foothills. The enemy transcendentally plays with their minds and mesmerizes the would-be liberators. Jake and his Lieutenant were first to receive pulsating lasers to the brain and wait motionless on horses for instruction. The powerful gorisilles very cautiously stay away from all water weapons.

A programmer instructs them in Beaulanish "Ride back to your superiors affirming concerns are frivolous, unfounded and not what you found here to be true!"

Another beast says, "You will all agree there are no hostages here. People are free to come and go as they please. We are peaceful immigrant homesteaders from a place called Fire Lake and only in need of wagons."

With that, the do-gooders ride out as if embarrassed for being wrong. Completely convinced, the folks standing on the scaffolds are painters. Once out of sight, the demons close the broken door. Charlie, Will, and another soldier remain in the cave. Hank is unseen and entirely unaware in the foothills tracking Cain.

Chapter 13

HEART AND SOUL

Hank and the Private lose Cain's trail before arriving to colder tribal land. Hunger calls them to warn Takoda's father, Chief Wiseoda, get something to eat and stay the night. Moving onward through tall grass, they spot some deeply scarred draft horses and mustangs grazing together.

They stop to let their mounts find nourishment on the lush grass for a while and rest themselves under an oak tree. The nearby herd suspiciously watches the two new horses grazing.

Hank asks, "What ya wanna bet the herd escaped slavery and that's why they're here?"

The Private says, "They're lucky! I hope all the indentured horses and folks get away soon! I wanted to open the corral at the factory. Time just never allowed for it Mr. Hank. What have these invaders been doing, sir?"

Hank says, "Not sure to guess why but they've been causing serious health issues for folks. Trying to ruin Beautyland will be the last thing they ever do!"

Continuing to higher aspen country, they sight an encampment in the midst of the forest. The landscape reveals splendorous views adorned with vibrant geysers and naturally pasteurized red dirt. A snow-white glacier overlaps a stream running past the horses.

The men advance into Indian Territory receiving countless smiles and greetings.

Chief Wiseoda hears the commotion and puts his arrow tools aside to meet the strangers. He wears a long eagle feathered headdress and turquoise adorned buckskin clothes.

The Chief joyously greets them with, "Hoh-do-ah-yu, hoh-do-ah-yu, gla-ah-se-tu, gla-ah-se-tu, hoh-do-ah-yu?"

The two Rangers introduce themselves and powwow. The teepee inside is decorated with turquoise beads and embroidered with significant Indian symbols. The moonlight pierces through and the firelight pierces out. Lush white, silver, black, brown, and golden fur blankets cover the floor with rawhide pillows adorning it. The post in the middle gleams with precious gems layered in wild game figures and spiritual symbols. A handcrafted beautifully decorated chestnut peace pipe sits on the floor. Eight braves sit in a ring around the post. The Rangers sit Indian-style to the right of the Chief. Hank and the soldier explain everything.

The Chief in turn recants, "Peace come, settle grudges, long ago! I write in book of legends."

His right hand holds a jewel laden buffalo-leather bound book. The thick parchment pages read in Indian Beaulanish. The cover reads, "Indian Lessons from Now to Then."

The Chief reads aloud tonight's inscription to the Rangers.

Day: Squirrel,
Month: Tree of Leaves Change,
Year: Vermin Wind,

"A bright white and red banded horse dances two steps back and rears in the moonlit sky.

It speaks with a loud havenly voice proclaiming, "Attention Beaulancians the Almighty God speaks through me, "Speak one language and conspire no mercy for the great disruptor. Beaulancia is a faithful unselfish serving nation. No tormentor can overtake the power of my protection. Defend yourselves without fear of wrongdoing. Evil seeks unjust death and complete destruction. You are of my Folkhaven they hate. We horses of grace are with you. Justice cometh – be not afraid."

Wiseoda looks up saying, "Then, horse vanish, poof, it gone!"

The Ranger's minds boggle in amazement. The Private says, "I hope to see this horse myself one time!"

Wiseoda pulls out a simple quill pen from a slot in the center post and enters more in the book, writing, *"We will obey this message." The conspirator is here. A Great Prophecy ending Blaze Evil will come true in Plentyville!"*

Hank says, "I have seen three mystical horses from Folkhaven. They will help us. We must eliminate this occupation for world peace to continue. The time has come to unite unto death!"

Long philosophical discussions drag on giving everyone much to contemplate.

Wiseoda says, "Squaws will overnight make water squirting skins. Braves will go beyond borders and leave the enemy in defeat."

Just then a young Indian boy places a platter of baked fish on a colorful blanketed setting on the floor of the teepee saying, "Eat, make strong!"

Four beautiful maidens deliver roasted turkey, corn on the cob, daisy greens salad, potatoes, three kinds of salsa, white cheese, flatbread, and an apple dumpling stew. The boy pours honey-sweetened mint tea into mugs from a clay pitcher and the chief raises one saying, "Victory for all Beaulancia (bew-lan-sha)!"

Hank and the Private eat as much of the feast as they can and retire into another warm teepee. Shining stars at the open top center relax them to sleep on snazzy fur laden ground. The camp sounds aloud in peaceful Indian song. Corralled horses chew hay, wind ruffles primitive shelters, and fires crack in pits. Both hard-rode Rangers listen and gently fall asleep.

Earlier, Jake's cluster of starry-eyed raiders galloped to the Commander in Chief's office and denied everything originally warned. Dulcets first thought was, *indeed.*

Nevertheless, he wired all military branches to take subsequent actions and dismissed the troopers back to Fort Intrepid. Jake and Ben are heading home. Charlie and Will were set free in a lost state of mind to go home.

Dulcet now sits behind his desk, scratching his head and thinking, *"What strangeness emerges, with incredible warnings and then the sudden calm? I feel a storm brewing. I ask for guidance, Lord. Give me the wisdom to interpret these peculiar events. I have never heard of Jake or anyone ever making such a mistake."*

He prays constantly for three uninterrupted hours. Sandra, the First Lady, enters the room, saying, "Dear, how are your pursuits evolving?"

The President says, "Oh, well, I suppose they are moving right along like the wind!"

He conceals the new story in half-truths but she does not fall for the passive voice and recognizes his troubled indifference exclaiming, "It just doesn't seem right!"

They adjourn to a breakfast nook in the kitchen and talk all night without sleep. Morning dew glistens on the kitchen bay window behind their table as the sun slowly rises.

Jake, Charlie, Will, and Ben reunite on the same trail going home in spell-stricken stupidity. They ride pleasantly alert horses atop a bluff over the polluted Blessing.

This is Scout's territory, and he is aware. He overlooks their movement perched on a tall redwood a mile away. He has been recruiting hawks, other eagles, condors, ravens, buzzards, storks, and even pelicans. They dive bomb anyone attempting to retrieve water. They take containers from people's hands and return them filled with freshwater. They save squirrels, minks, mice, rabbits, raccoons, skunks, foxes, native-lizards, snakes and more. They even retrieve fish and transfer them to the unspoiled waters in the northern quadrant.

During the intervening period, Cain comes back to the plant and waits on slaves readying new wagons for transport back to Relief Island. Blaze is cracking a whip there on three previously seized farmers, shouting: "No one slumbers!" You work or you die!"

Meanwhile, Molly toils with a sledgehammer alongside other slaves in breaking boulders to stones. Lizards crawl around her legs drooling for a bite. An aurora illuminating off her boots signals to them an electric shock if they try. Astro had cast a protective barrier around her and all the captive slaves in a snorted wind. He and a mustang now pull a loaded buckboard to a hatch on one of the many center volcanos. This one, Blaze calls, "Bertha!"

The construction of this tall smokestack and many others is nearly complete. All cones point toward Beautyland and deadly gases will eventually fumigate it.

The demons are plugging fiery volcanic pools with tons and tons of salted sulfur rock. It clogs throats and pressurizes cores enough to explode. Sulfur Dioxide gas will blast out cone heads and north winds will blow the smog across Beauty. Evil's inductees will continue feeding the infernos until it occurs.

Undersea volcanic seepage is emerging into the ocean with precipitating mineral deposits rich in iron, copper, arsenic, zinc, and platinum. Warm springs rich in sulfur rise to the surface and provide nourishment for the damned. Blaze will keep the SO_2 blowing over Beauty Land for as long as it takes to kill everyone. When the final catastrophic phase begins two thousand manlike beasts and two thousand pit bulls will ship out aboard the enormous platinum freighter ready for war. Nearly the same amount will stay behind to defend the Island. The vessel will soar at full steam ahead and land a physical assault on Beautyland.

The ship's buoyancy performs exceptionally well under heavy loads. Evil uses slag from smelting operations for ballast. The vessel has cabins equipped with sulfur baths. The demons enjoy cleaning up with hydrogen sulfide. To them the rotten egg scent is a perfume. The four-tiered craft holds two fuel tanks filled with flammables from Evil's own refinery. On the top deck are two private cabins, one for Blaze and one for Cain. Platinum does not tarnish but many slaves on board volunteer to sweep it to a shine otherwise the vessel's decks would be filthy. Stalls in the hold on the second tier from the bottom are made of salvaged planks from Evil's original wreckage. Captured mustangs and humans wait there during transport. They stand beside pallets containing pressurized cylinders of liquid sulfur dioxide (SO_2) used to feed the Lava Clan. It turns water into sulfuric acid and spices up their crunchy coal and mud for gravy.

The hold also carries yellow blocks of uranium ore and white phosphorus. The garlic smell suffocates some passengers. The mechanical room is in the stern on the first level past the galley and in the forward are bunk beds for beasts. The third tier up holds more crew below the main deck.

The millions of flies swarming the ocean liner stagger beasts as well. It is part of their condemnation. Confiscated peanuts and watermelons store on board with kelp as food for man and horse. The melons distribute water safely to hostages without the Lava Clan having to touch it. Twice a day after meals the confined must throw buckets of putrid acid on the decks and tables to rinse juice down drains into the sea. The demons take no chances in contact with it. Blaze Evil's progress over the centuries has been dramatic.

He proudly boasts, "I am the master!"

He actually believes he has the power to defeat Strong Am's resistance.

He says, "Soon all Beauty will be mine to un-bless!"

He perpetuates his own worship deducing a conquest is within his rights. He thinks it is only fair for surviving the exile so long. He believes Strong Am respects him as a match. The very thought is an abomination to the entire Folkhaven Kingdom. They invented natural resources for better use than means of destruction.

At midday, the Lava Clan stops working to kneel before two deified images. Both stand as ten-foot-tall platinum statues on a hillside pedestal. One resembles an elderly likeness of Strong Am with long hair,

beard, and a toga draped over a shoulder. The other is a black iron likeness of Blaze. It stands slightly behind Strong Am smiling with a hand
on His shoulder. Using ultra-intense lasers, he shaped his own likeness
stronger in physique.

Blaze stands on the hill now in front of his worshippers giving a sermon saying, "I am better than the so-called One True God!"

They bow in remembrance of the fate befalling those who argue. He
lifts a vile of fresh watermelon juice as a threat. Astro snapped out of the
trance soon after the ship left the pier at the coast. His spiritual connection
to the Folkhavens is stronger than any spell Blaze could ever place. During
the voyage over in the ship's hold, he waved his versatile mane over Molly's
eyes and freed her from the hocus-pocus. This morning he pulls a cart on
the Island with another mustang uphill to a square hatch in the middle of
a smokestack, singing, "Hi-de-ho, hi-de-hay, tomorrow's not a rainy day!
Hi-de ho, hi, de, hum, neither is today, ba-bum, ba-bum, ba-bum!"

A brute whips them to go faster saying, "Only a few more dumps and
this volcano will be done."

After dropping compounds into stack hatches the boiling lava accu-
mulates combustible gas and explosions force out cones into prevailing
winds.

Astro asks his tugging companion, "How is the biz, honey?"

She responds, "If these jackals would ever be quiet for just a minute,
I will tell you. There must be thousands of them here. Why don't they
just keep quiet?"

She shakes her long blonde mane over her ears to muff out the barking racket.

Astro says, "I will sing."

She says, "I hope I never make it to another incinerator chute. I
would rather die than help Evil do this."

Astro says, "The stacks spit giant fireballs at Beautyland clogging the
sky with smog."

Her yellow tail arches up in disgust behind a creamy yellow and sable
pinto frame.

She asks, "How long must we endure?"

Astro says, "Sugar honey, hang on!"

She says, "I know I'm not delightful."

He says, "Not at this time, but you will be, have faith!"

She sarcastically but sweetly says, "Time is my worst enemy."

He says, "You would like the place where I am from. Time is plentiful without deadlines!"

They strenuously pull uphill and she cannot figure out where he gets the energy to keep going. She is starving, dehydrated, and ready to collapse. Two rations of watermelon per day do not cut it for her. Whippings occur every few minutes and they work nonstop, yet most of the time he is singing.

She asks herself, *"What is it with this guy? He never tires?"*

Her head points down and her ears stiffen straight back while she begrudgingly pulls using all of her might. Astro pulls while performing another song-and-dance routine. He whoops out, "Oh when the saints, oh when the saints, oh when the saints go marching in. Oh, would you like to be in that number, when the saints go marching in? "Oh, when the saints, oh when the saints, oh when the saints go marching in! da-da-da-da, da-da, da-da, da da-da, da-da-da-da"

He sings the same song repeatedly as lashing whips attack their backs and dogs snap at their hocks. The beastly wagon driver shouts, "Gargies giddy diyap, slouve on, and no 'yime sor mir pazy shoofers," meaning, 'hurry!'

He swats the mare into gear.

She asks Astro, "Who are these saints you keep going on about and when are they going to march in?"

Astro says, "Well, if you will tell me who you are, I will give an account to you."

She says, "Me! I am Colima."

Astro says, "Well, Colima, hmm, I like that! Why are you called Colima?"

She says, "Is it not obvious?"

Astro replies, "No!"

She says, "Look at my side and under my belly."

He turns to get a glimpse and says, "Oh yes! It is as beautiful as your face. So why are you called Colima?"

She answers, "The Indians named me that. The big greenish oval marking looks like a lime. It means with lime."

Astro looks again and laughs, "Huh, ha ha heh he heh heh he heh heh!"

"What's so funny?" she asks?

Astro explains, "I see the lime. I get it! What a pretty lime. You have many sweeter fruits about you though, Ms. Colima."

She replies, "Yes, I do, but that is enough about me. Tell me who the saints are and when they are going to march in, Mr. Toothy Fruity!"

Astro says, "Yes, indeed! I am Astro, but you may call me Astry."

She answers, "Nice to meet you, Astry."

He admits, "Thanks, it is a privilege to pull alongside you and here is the scoop. There are two other celestial steeds like me. One is my genius brother Spirit and the other is my cousin Utopio, a majestically handsome stallion. They do not have my singing voice but we are all on a mission from God."

She responds, "Oh right, you're saying the other two are going to march in? Whom are you trying to fool? You are no saint. Are they going to march in anytime soon? You had better tell me the truth. I am not going to help pull this cart no matter how hard I am beaten if you don't."

Astro replies, "I am, I am, just listen. Do not get tart. I am not squeezing your lime, Colima! I cannot divulge everything, but I am answering your questions. Do not worry. I am telling you the truth."

He makes it clear that the other two march on Beautyland at this very moment.

She asks, "Do you mean it?"

He says, "I am absolutely sure of it. Do not let the torture crack you. It will soon end, little citrus cutie, uh-huh, uh-huh!"

She snorts and whinnies, but his adorable smile reveals a calmness that ensures belief. Somehow, his kind eyes overwhelm all doubts and silence her curiosities. For a moment, peace follows until the fiend snaps his lash on their backs again and in unison both move faster singing, "Oh, when the saints, oh when the saints, oh when the saints, 'come,' marching in, da-da-da-da, da-da-da-da, da-da-da-da-da-da-da-da. . ."

Another rawhide thong slashes the air before the growly demonic voice of Blaze yells, "Pick it up! Pick it up! Reload that vehicle!"

Molly is in a quarry painfully distributing her sledgehammer against stubborn boulders. Forceful ferocious dogs and beasts guard her activity with whips and growling smiles. She toils in sweat before sunup and adds a shovel load to a half-empty cart. She thinks of escape, *I have to get out of here! O my Beautyland, how I long to be home. I feel like a traitor. I cannot continue much longer. My heart aches for you. Is there no one who can stop this madness?"*

An overly zealous beast cracks a whip saying, "Load the cart, you lazy sloth."

Chapter 14

REVITALIZING

Sunrise displays brown ashy clouds on the horizon. Will wakes first on a ridge over the Blessing. Jake, Ben, and Charlie continue snoozing in the camp. Scout is near and concerned to see the lazy men sleeping on this ridge. He watches from a tree across the Blessing saying to himself, *"Strange, to sleep, past sunup, mission not done up. To be on this range at this time is strange! I will swoop down with a frown."*

He bolts off the branch and glides nine hundred feet in updrafts to land on an alligator juniper branch in camp. Will startles as Scout flaps wings to signal his presence. He stands staring at the eagle from only seventeen feet away. Scout notices the reaction and bobs his strong white head up and down in friendship. Will bends down to reach the coffee pot off the fire saying to himself,

"I think this strange eagle is talking to me?"

He looks again at the bird while sipping and says, "Come here, eagle. Come to me. You are a handsome fella! I won't hurt ya, talk to me. Do you like beans? Come here and I will give you some."

Scout jumps to the ground and walks within kicking range while staring into Will's eyes. The wrangler stares back in speechless awe. Scout says with wings in sign language, *"Don't drink from the river or spring, they are polluted."*

Will replies, "No, they are not, it was only a hoax put on by some ill-humored folks. It is not true. Do not worry eagle. The water is fine."

Scout answers, *"Sweiserrt, sweiserrt,* I am Scout! Scout is out! I know what the water is all about! Do not you doubt! *Sweiserrt,* drink and you will find out, *sweiserrt, sweiserrt!"*

He looks closer at the wrangler's eyes saying, "Hmm, too many wineskins are danger Ranger. Wine cause male to totter off trail."

"What wineskins?" asks Will?

Scout points to the tack on the ground saying, "Those skins at the saddle dump, bumpkin!"

"Oh, no, those are water skins. I ain't had any wine," Will answers.

Scout adds, "Too much you drink, I think."

Will agrees, "Yes," with a big grin on his face.

Scout asks, "Why so big and many, by yiminny?"

Will answers, "Ah well, it's been warm, and we get thirsty. Uh, we do have a heavy load, all right, I do not know why. I suppose we are a long way from home."

"Where are you going not knowing?" asks Scout.

Will looks at the other Rangers sleeping and says, "Uh, home?"

"How far is home to roam?" asks Scout.

Will replies, "Let me see, hmm, about a thousand miles I'd say."

Scout asks, "Where home issy, Mr. Dizzy? It is so far from here, to go, I dare? Lad is you sure you had no wine, no time?"

"No, we live on an island far across the sea," says Will.

Scout looks very deeply into his eyes and points a wing at the loaded skins, asking, "Mouthpiece with big nozzle is for ease to squirt fleas, huh?"

He suspiciously stares the man down. Will is dazed, takes his hat off and scratches his head in confusion. Scout zones in, with eagle eye penetration and signals him to come closer. He transfixes on his pupils and shouts, "Demons are eating your sleeping friends!"

Will laughs, "Uh-ha!"

Scout asks, "You help not?"

"The demons are our friends. They wouldn't eat anyone," Will assures.

Now the worried Scout passes between his legs over to Jake snoring on a blanket. He nudges him with a talon until he awakes and looks close into his blank eyes. He projects a notorious eagle squint casting predator wisdom deep into Jake's brain. He sees a dead zone within and says, "Spellbound, from a beast goes around? Fix your eyes on mine and you will unwind!"

He hops on his chest to look straight at him from only an inch away and commences a transcending stare. He spins pupils sending pulsations into Jake's memory to cut out a noticeable radioactive red line.

Jake suddenly jumps off the ground, pushing Scout aside yelling, "Where am I? What am I doing here?"

He flies to Will's shoulder sending pulsations into his eyes until he snaps out of it and leaps over to cure Ben and lastly Charlie. They rise to their senses. Scout lifts above the camp onto a pine branch and overlooks a frantic discussion. Jake holds his head in his hands, asking, "What are we doing here?"

Charlie understands the confusion on everyone's face saying,

"The beasts cast a spell on all of us. I thought it was only Will and me. I can't understand how they did it but I do remember going blank."

Ben says, "Yeah, I do too."

Charlie says, "Look, smoke signals!"

Will sees the signals in the sky above Scout and says, "Jake, it's an urgent warning from Takoda."

He sees the streaming smoke line from Mount Harmony and realizes Takoda is requesting aide

Jake says, "Charlie, go to Dulcet and explain our failures at the warehouse."

"I am on my way," he replies.

In wasting no time, he saddles up and kicks out to a run over the plateau as fast as possible. The others saddle up and race toward the signals. Halfway to the Mount in the woods Takoda approaches waving a feathered tomahawk above his long black hair. No one speaks until getting very close for fear of who may be around.

Takoda explains, "I saw monster dog, lead pack, go your ranch. I know family alone. I look for Saber Toes to help me follow. I not see him and find you. You speak to President yet?"

Jake agrees, "Yes, indeed! Come with us, Takoda. We have new weapons. Take this sack, point and squeeze. It is only water, but it will melt them down."

He hands the spare and Takoda puts straps overhead hanging it in underarm position. He test squeezes a blast at a weed and uproots it from the ground.

"I like, follow me. I lead you home safe," he declares.

Before long, Saber Toes joins them running up alongside.

In the distance out of sight, twenty drooling dogs follow Lucer across a footbridge before Goodman's ranch. Lady runs from under the porch, barking at the incomers. On second thought, she smells them and turns back under the porch. Max sees the varmints from a window and warns Judy and Kristin washing lunch dishes. They hear the mongrels and frantically grab rifles to take positions at open windows.

Danny Boy smells dogs outside and rouses other animals to awareness. The horses kick stalls open and congregate at the back of the barn. Danny Boy and Daisy bust through the wall with reared walloping hooves and escape to the apple orchard with Mirabelle and the sheep. Violet, Freckles, and Pop-Up run to the chicken coop. Violet looks it over saying, "Pop-Up, get inside with the chickens, y'all is much safer there than out in the open."

He does to the dismay of the roosters but finds a soft barren spot in a far corner and digs a hole, murmuring, "Bad doggies, yepsir bad, bad doggies, I got ta dig, a deep, deep hole."

Chickens watch from bedded shelves. Freckles the strawberry roan puts her teeth to the pigpen door and releases the latch saying,

"Come on, little piggy's if you want to grow into big hogs someday you better follow us!"

One momma, three piglets, and a hog rush out snorting behind Freckles to the apple orchard. The ferocious gargie platoon barks and snarls at the farms main entrance. Max fires a shotgun into one's eyes from the living room window and blinds it. The gargie leans into barbed wire connected to the front gate and scrambles with paws over eyes until securely hooked.

Max shouts, "I got him, the tramp's lights are out."

The dog mutters, "Grr. . . owlie, gruff, grrrufff," and blindly rips away from the wire only to stagger back to the bridge where he falls in the creek and dies. Danny Boy, Violet, and Daisy dash in to fight from the orchard. They charge at a few in the yard with rears and bucks and manage to put several to shame. The horses fight with speed and agility as never before.

<hr>

Saber Toes arrives before the Rangers to save Violet. He lunges at one about to jump on her back striking its face and boxes another faster than it can see. He plucks eyeballs rendering them helpless. Danny Boy kicks three gargie jackals over the fence outside the yard. The lava clan gargies get their senses knocked out and remain motionless but alive.

Lucer and the other gargies make way against bullets toward the house. Kristin shoots through the window and blinds a few. Lucer rages on up the front stairs with muscular legs and breaks the door down. The family fires in vain. His mouth slips a metal tooth across Judy's right bicep.

Her gun falls to the floor as an infantry horn blows from the footbridge. Lucer runs and jumps out the window to the porch.

Jake and the gang finally arrive. They blast dead the motionless gargies first. Will plays the bugle repeatedly as Saber Toes leaves for the hills. Lucer leaps from the porch to the yard snarling and staring down the Rangers. Danny Boy, Violet, and Daisy stand watching. Two beasty gargies form a roadblock. Ben hits hard with repeating squirts dropping them to a sizzling death. Takoda kills two more. The squirts turn them into steaming ooze as Goodman's family watches from the living room with fast beating hearts.

Will shouts, "Oh no, you don't!" and shoots one about to take a chunk of his leg.

Ben cries, "Take this, you varmint," with every shot he takes.

Horse hooves knock the ground like sledgehammers and plunder the grass with swooping, cracking, and crunching. Melting gargie carcasses cover the yard sizzling with moans. Jake squirts a zapping stream at a husky tiger-striped beast in front of Lucer. The skirmish winds down as Will kills three more.

Jake races beside the house after Lucer and five other gargies guarding his flank. He kills all but Lucer, the skedaddling alpha dog. Another few exit out the main gate only to be herded by Takoda and Will into the readily killing creek. Lucer leaps over the barbed wire fence far west of the house and bolts out of sight. Jake does not see him run to trees along the creek and double back to the bridge. He turns around on the other side looking at the house and laughing like a hyena with snout to the sky, three times, as if to say, "It's not over!"

He turns toward the spring and runs into the southern hills where Saber Toes watches his every move. Judy bleeds but is alive on the living room floor. Kristin attends to her by applying pressure to the wound with a clean wet cloth. The men dismount and tie their horses to the hitching post at the porch.

Jake enters and kisses Judy, saying, "Honey, I am so sorry I didn't get here sooner. Wake up, babe! Wake up! Please wake up."

Takoda squats beside Judy, peels the cloth away, sniffs, and says, "Humph, metal!"

He pulls a piece of splintered tooth from the cut and says,

"Poison metal in blood, body stiff, stomach swollen, she need throw out mouth. We get all metal out or she die, whole body sick. She hot, you take to bed and wipe cold water. I get shaman, he fix. I hurry. I back soon!"

Without another word, Takoda leaves across the creek riding north-west toward Indian Country. He travels far quickly. Kristin managed to get Judy to throw up in a large bowl and that brought down the fever and some swelling, but her temperature is still high. Jake and Will carry her to bed. Max brings in cold wet cloths. Will and Max leave the bedroom while Jake and Kristin strip Judy and wipe her face continuously trying to bring down the fever. Ben is outside rounding up the livestock. Will and Max go outside to help. They find the broken-down wall in the barn and start rebuilding it.

Ben sees Max and says, "Hey, I am putting the animals in the corral. Is that all right with you?"

Max answers, "Sure, and thanks!"

Ben does not know about Pop-Up but the rabbit will find a way out of the coop. That is for sure even if he has to chew his way out. Ben feeds the animals some special treats from the palm of his hand. They calm down with reassurances. It is still too early for dinner, so Ben cleans the stalls.

Jake addresses Kristin in the bedroom, saying, "Honey, I want to sit with your mother. The men worked hard today, and I bet they are get-ting hungry."

Kristin says, "I am sure they are, Dad. I am so glad to see you home again, safe and sound. I will fix something up for all of you."

She hugs her dad beside Judy on the bed and goes straight to the kitchen to prepare coffee, fried chicken, mashed potatoes, green beans, biscuits, gravy, and "Apple Betty" for dessert.

Jake rubs Judy's forehead with the cold wet cloth, saying, "Babe, I love you. If you come out of this, I will build the new house just the way you want it. Wake up. As soon as the war ends, the house is sure as built. Honey, I missed my chance to save you. I am so sorry! I am here now to protect you, honey! I will not leave you alone again. I'll never leave you alone honey. Wake up, darlin'! We need you! All of us do. I need you, sweetheart! You can't die, sweetheart!"

Jake looks at the wound and sobs with tears flowing profusely down his face and pleads again, "You can't die, sweetheart. Wake up! Please wake up! I love you, Judy. We all love you, honey. Please wake up!"

The cool blue skies in the mountains depict good weather. Takoda roams fast and scares a herd of grazing elk. In loping another mile, he sees smoke. It looks like a campfire. He gradually approaches to get a good look and finds the tribal shaman.

"Mistappi, Mistappi! How Mistappi, I search for you, Mistappi."

The medicine man is brewing a potion and says, "Ug, me wait for you, why so slow? I know you seek Mistappi. I have vision in stream. I sit and watch rapids flow. Great Spirit flattens stream to quiet waters. Image of woman appear, on floor, and you kneel. Mud floats on glassy image and woman rises. I know then what cure woman. I know you look for me. I come here for you. I make potion with clay. Here, hold pouch!"

Mistappi hands Takoda a large leather bag. He scoops in fifty pounds of dry gray clay from a pile off the ground and says, "Take this back to woman. Make much mud, cover whole body and head. Do not drown, let breathe, she stay in mud. Rise in one day."

Takoda warmly thanks the shaman and excitedly hurries back. After only a few twists through the forest, he hears another rider breaking branches and stomping ferns.

A voice calls, "Hold up. It's me, Chokwok!"

Takoda asks, "Great warrior, what are you doing here?"

Chokwok answers, "We find Hank lost in forest."

Takoda sees and replies, "Hank, my wrangler friend."

Hank explains, "The Private and I lost their leader in the foothills beyond the wagon factory. We left your father's land to do reconnaissance toward the spring. Only we got lost. We are only safe thanks to Chokwok."

Chokwok asks, "What Takoda say I do with them?"

Takoda explains, "Warn all tribes to prepare weapons of water. I take two friends with me."

Chokwok insists, "Show me skin. OK! I see how to work it. I go make all tribes ready."

Takoda adds, "The Maukegan's, good friends with Shashouix, We go, must help Jake's wife at ranch now!"

The children and men are eating dessert solemnly back at the ranch as Takoda's team arrives. It startles them as he dashes inside the house, shouting, "Jake, where is she, where is Jake?"

Kristin answers, "He is in the bedroom with Mom."

"Okay, I wait here," Takoda replies.

Jake comes out, asking, "Takoda, what have you got?"

Takoda answers, "I have potion, she well in one day."

Jake insists, "Great, give it to me!"

Takoda replies, "Not ready, make mud first."

The others ask, "Mud?"

Jake asks, "Mud, is that what you said?"

Takoda declares, "Yes, Jake, hurry, make lots of mud, for bath. Wife lay in mud, take poison out."

Without delaying, Jake asks everyone except Kristin to help. They notice Hank and the Private leading horses to the barn. The men are ecstatic but have no time to talk.

Jake instructs Kristin, "Prepare the tub."

She races to the back porch, removes a canvas cover from an oblong metal basin on casters, and rolls it into Judy's room. Max manually pumps the well while Ben fills a bucket under the faucet. Jake, Takoda, and Will dig up dirt and shovel it into two large wheelbarrows. Ben pours bucket after bucket into them.

Takoda insists, "More! More!"

He gets the medicine pouch off his saddle and pours half into each wheelbarrow. Will stir's vigorously.

"Enough," says Takoda.

Jake takes hold of a wheelbarrow and charges alone to the house. He pulls it up the porch stairs by himself and trudges along to the bedroom. Kristin, with all of her might and Jake lift Judy's limp body into the bathtub. Jake tilts the barrow to the rim and pours mud all over her gowned body. Takoda brings the second wheelbarrow in with Ben and Will. They shovel the contents over her. Takoda rubs the mud into her hair and covers her face deeply. She breathes and Takoda remarks, "That done. Now we wait!"

Kristin invites him to sit at the table for a wholesome meal. Ben and Will haul the wheelbarrows back outside and greet Hank and the Private while Max feeds the livestock. The reunited Rangers have much to talk over. They enter the house and join Takoda at the table, where they get a wholesome meal. Hank shares his experiences and Jake knows he is there. Judy remains his biggest concern. He is glad to know Hank is fine and will catch up later. He kneels beside Judy's oblong tub, holding her hand. His head bends down in prayer. She blinks.

Chapter 15

BATTLE STATIONS

Table talk exasperates Kristin's patience when learning the where-abouts of the havenly steeds. Hank gave her an idea. While the crew, Max, and her father slumber, she leaves a note and sneaks outside to the barn speaking to Violet, "Come here, girl. We are going for a ride," and outfits the black mare complete with saddlebags and rations. A water gun hanging by a horseshoe hook on a wall gets her attention. She takes it down fastens the shoulder straps over the saddle horn, and leads Violet out by the reins. She latches the barn door closed behind and mounts steering toward the back forty acres in a slow walk. Once far enough away, she kicks to top speed up a rugged hill heading north to find Utopio. The black horse in the dark night blends except for Kristin's long blonde hair under a pink plaid patriot hat. They pass trees and discreetly climb more hills into Beaver Country. High in the blue sky at sunrise, between green hills and clear lakes, a red-tailed hawk glides overhead, screeching. Kristin sees the dam forming under the new bridge.

Hundreds of beavers swim diligently in the shrinking Blessing fitting logs from mouths into slots on the foundation. A giant lake is forming at the top. The dam's construction is under Spirit's supervision, and Utopio stands stoutly atop the framing bridge.

Kristin shouts, "Topio, Topio, hello, hello!"

He jumps off with dragonfly grace and lands head-to-head with Violet.

"Emmerrahh," he whinnies and nudges up to Kristin's treat filled hands.

She whimpers, "Our ranch was invaded. My mom is sick. Terrible creatures raided us."

Utopio speaks her language, saying, "I am on it, Kristin. Cross over to my back!"

She does by grabbing onto his red mane tightly and tells Violet, "Go home, girl, you'll do fine without me. You can eat along the way!"

Violet raises her head and Kristin kisses her purple nose. She puts the water gun over a shoulder, removes the bit and bridle to a saddlebag and sends Violet home.

Utopio asks, "Are you on?"

He lifts all four legs off the ground.

She answers, "Topio, take it easy. I can feel your strong pulse. I feel supercharged. Wait do not go yet. I need a moment to adjust. Are we going to fly?"

Her body repositions forward with arms around Utopio's neck.

She declares, "I am on an angel and my skin is all lit up. My hair is glistening. I am not scared! I am on an angel!"

Her sparkling kind blue eyes look at Spirit as Utopio rears off in flaming slow speed above Spirit's head. He lands again atop the bridge and loudly says to all, "I am leaving to take Kristin home, and after, I will finish the tunnel."

The beavers bid him farewell with chattering teeth and squeaky grunts. Spirit responds with a long three-whinny regard.

"Whinny whinny whinnieiey!"

Topio understands him to say, "Be safe, kick butt, and I will see you soon!"

Utopio rears up again into the sky and turns in midair off the bridge. The falls decrease as beavers pack quicklime mortar between lumber spaces. As soon as Utopio finishes the tunnel under the spring, sending water into the reservoir, other duties will keep him even busier. Utopio sees Scout zooming up and down in the River gorge dodging red flashes and hitting oxidized ironstone walls with his beak. Utopio is perplexed and asks himself, *"What should I do, risk Kristin's life to save Scout or take her home first?"*

He decides, for the sake of the human child to leave Scout to divine providence. The eagle must wait. Utopio zips away in super mighty form to the ranch. At the barn, he gently bends to ground and Kristin slides off his fibrous back. Before the sound of her next breath, Utopio is four thousand yards away. Just as Scout is about to fall into the River, Utopio arrives and swoops him up in his teeth. Scout clasps the long mane with his talons as a red laser from a demonic staff intersects puncturing his stomach.

Utopio lands him on a ledge and the knocked-out bird will not wake up. Utopio dashes away toward the assailants. Cain is about to cross a bridge over the Blessing with captives and a wild bunch of gorisilles. Utopio stops and floats in midair undisguised against the sunlight to investigate the marauders.

They drive new empty wagons and slaves to the dock for reloading at the warehouse. When the loading is complete, the slaves will shove off on the platinum ship to the island.

Utopio is perplexed again and asks himself, *"What should I do, stay and fight them off or help Scout first? I'll check on Scout, it's not over."*

He whinnies angelically strong throughout the canyon. Cain roars back like a lion. Their echoes repeat toward the coast as Scout lies stiff, and Utopio drops a tear on him saying, "Get up my friend. Can you hear me? I said get up!"

More tears fall, "Scout, let my tears soak in! Hear my voice, Get up!"

He blows streams of mystically enhanced air from his nostrils to Scout's beak and the eagle moves not. "I must leave you now, ol' buddy, but I will be back. I promise! I will be back. I know you will get up soon all better and unafraid. You are Scout! You know what it is about. I have to go now but you stay here. Do not worry. I'll be back for you."

He drifts lightly in the breeze to the spring upriver while sniffing and shaking his eyes, thinking, *"Aha, a hiding place in the arroyo by the spring. Lucer and the other guards will not distinguish me from a fall-colored maple. I will sneak up to the spring's entrance impersonating a gargie."*

The guard hands him a bone shaped sulfuric treat, saying, "Get on down to the mouth of the aquifer. Your shift has started."

Topio walks like a dog past him to the bottom of the shaft. Gorisilles mix chemicals turning water yellow as it flows over a five-foot wide trough and drops out a spout only inches above the River.

Topio can hardly stand the stench and drops the bone. He dives into the spring's eye and transforms into a gigantic snake with teeth as heavy as cannons. The sharp twisted pointed teeth render easy digging better than any man made drill. He chomps out chunks of earth and plugs the waterway into the cavern.

He cuts through rocky underground creating a new watercourse beside the River. It is a long and wide diversion. He doubles back to the cavern's riverside spout and seals it spitting in muddy rocks. At the same time, Spirit is tightening the dam so the river will quickly shrink. Utopio drills to the far arroyo where Cain shot Scout. He reroutes the underground stream through the banks of the ravine, looks at the splashes gushing up and says, *"Oops, I don't know my own strength,"* and quickly plugs the break.

He dives deeper into the aquifer, crosses under the river and continues drilling, until finally reaching the low land near the lone Elm as planned. He spits dirt off his tongue as the water bursts onto the meadow and rises away as a horse again. He watches the water fill the land thinking,

"I did a good job. This beats anything I have ever done, no brag just fact, uh, ha, whinny," and rears in the sky looking like a flame from the sun.

He sees captives, demons, and buckboards below. Cain rides the beautiful Appaloosa over the Harmony Bridge crossing the Blessing. Utopio knows Jake has been to the President and gone home again. He feels obligated to report these findings to Dulcet and darts away with newly found mighty horsepower.

In the city, Charlie rides up the wide brick boulevard under shady trees to the Mansions main gate. He has only just arrived and knows the story has to be, believed! Dulcet took everyone for an idiot when Jake's men told him all was well. This will be Charlie's day of reckoning. The first call to arms directly and unequivocally confused Dulcet. The guards allow passing through the gate alone to the house. He hitches up to a post and bangs the large brass loop on the door, thinking, "*how strange, no guards here.*"

The door opens and a hand reaches out welcoming him. The Commander in Chief says, "Charlie, it's you, come in!"

Charlie steps inside explaining last night's hypnosis to him in the foyer.

"The original warnings were true," he says.

Charlie notices the President acting strange and says, "I know you must be exhausted and confused Mr. President? Please listen to the whole story."

Charlie understands well how Dulcet would not know what to believe or whom to trust anymore. Still, his strange response is surprising. He puts his hand out to shake and the President grips tightly not letting go. Charlie hears something coming from the room on the right behind a draped entrance sounding like clunky pattering feet running across the floor. Charlie does not wait to ask and shoves Dulcet loose. He pulls his water gun forward into firing position and dashes into the room. A fat two-legged black hairy beast wearing chemically speckled dog-skin over-alls looks back at him from halfway out of the rear window. His spiraling red eyes look dangerous. Charlie aims and the brute quickly falls out the window before he can fire. Charlie hurries over to watch it jump a rock wall and run past thick weeds to a cornfield near the Harmony Bridge. It keeps low to the ground like an ape.

He looks at Dulcet and explains shouting quickly, "Cain is Blaze Evils' son! He and his goons are ready to annihilate us. Why didn't you tell me one was in there?"

The President responds, "One what, an invader, hehhehheh!"

Charlie replies, "This is no hoax. Round up our troops. This is war, Dulcet!"

He stares looking into the Commander in Chief's eyes.

"Hmm, you look dazed, not exhausted. Hmm, Mr. President, why don't we just go to your office and I will send out for a nice cake."

Charlie takes him by the hand, and the President responds,

"Oh, I would enjoy that. Yes, let us sit and have some cake and coffee too! I do so like cake and coffee, how about you, Mr. Cavanaugh?"

They walk across the hall, and Dulcet sits down looking very happy behind the great desk.

Charlie responds, "Mr. President! I would like you to reinstall me in command of the B.L. Navy. I will assume all necessary decisions to protect our great land at sea. I will control all maritime activities for the further good of our shores."

The Commander in Chief dazedly replies, "Good man! What a wonderful idea. We may then have the coffee and cake to celebrate your loyal gallantry. I do enjoy your forthright ambition for the land, my man."

Charlie quickly interrupts, "No, sir. Jake has the land. I take the sea."

Dulcet agrees, "All right, there you have it, sir! By Harmonious delight another great Beaulancian has risen! I am glad to have you aboard, Admiral, Commandant or whatever. I will also appoint Mr. Goodman to five-star general status, yes sir, good man, that Goodman!"

"Indeed, Mr. President, Jake Goodman is then the new five-star general," says Charlie.

Dulcet replies, "Now Cavanaugh, sir, where is that cake? Let us celebrate. Oops, I mean Admiral Cavanaugh, sir."

Charlie, not surprised understands his affliction and insinuates, "Mr. President, you are floating on a trip in hypnosis but you will be glad you were when this is over."

He finds unharmed servants hiding in the kitchen and orders a slice of cake and coffee delivered to Dulcet in the office within a minute.

Charlie explains, "Jake did already assume the position as top-ranking General, Mr. President."

Dulcet acknowledges, "Of course he did. Well then, now he is Secretary of Defense!"

Charlie coaxes The President to administer authentic writs with Beautyland's official insignia stamped on signed parchment for both himself and Jake. The mandate orders Charlie's enlistment as the supreme Admiral over all maritime authorities. The President signs it as the cake enters with a waiter carrying a full silver, serving platter.

Charlie asks the President to excuse him for a minute and slips out the front door. He finds four guards at the bottom of the stairs lying in hedges deader than skunks on a road. Utopio suddenly appears on the lawn. Charlie explains everything he encountered, as does Utopio in his own native tongue. He snorts, bobs, dances, points his red tail, motions with his snout for Charlie to mount and says, "I will fly you to the fleet at the port."

Charlie wastes no time deciding and jumps on. Utopio ascends without wings or fancy feathers. He just rises to any speed from any point even faster than the speed of light if so chosen. His coat is so versatile it can turn invisible. They arrive at the port. Charlie dismounts on a huge wooden dock with four ships on each side and takes charge.

Utopio zooms again across the sky to the fort and greets cavalry horses in a large barn. They have suspicions at first but soon listen. He explains the Appaloosa and the enslaved mustangs. They stand in military horse attention listening to every word.

A large bay with a white strip on his face asks, "How can we help? Soldiers don't listen to horses."

A Buckskin gelding says, "Mine does!"

Utopio has a plan and flies outside onto the main yard of the enclosed fort. In front of the headquarters building, he stands stoutly in view. The troopers think it is a fire about to spread and run outside from all doors around the compound.

The still-dazed Lieutenant in recuperation sees him and says,

"I am under a spell. No, I am not. Yes, I am. No, I am not! Wait I am having an epiphany. I rather remember Jake talk, who is Jake? Anyway, it was about a flamboyant horse like you."

Utopio replies, "No worries something is gradually wearing off you Lieutenant. Like a brain cloud!"

The Lieutenant remembers the ride from the stables to the wagon factory, saying, "I heard Charlie mention you. You're the fiery stud who knows Jake, and he knows you too. You are Topio! Where's ya cousins fella? Are they working on the Dam? Ben told me, you know Ben. Who is Ben?"

Utopio backs up as the Lieutenant stumbles in a swagger. He gains control, saying, "I'm all right fella. Tell me why you are here. Why are you here, boy?"

At that moment, a wrangling corporal lays a loop over Utopio's neck. He thinks again in an instant as Utopio burns the lasso through in less than one second. The soldiers are astonished. The Lieutenant scolds the man and touches Utopio's neck in friendship. He moves in closer and rubs a cheek saying, "Easy, boy, easy, tell us why you are here. I didn't tell that idiot to do that!"

Utopio releases a whinny with forceful representation and says,

"I am on a mission from Strong Am to stop Evil. He is stockpiling weapons of mass destruction and wants to pollute every watershed. The Lava Clan has enslaved Beaulancians to help further annihilate you and all of Beautyland. You must prepare an orderly readiness for battle.

"Go east across Eagle Bridge and follow the old mining trail north until you find the Salt Dome Caverns at the coastal road intersection. Do not look into enemy eyes. Use water skins to extinguish them. The Evils have munitions enough to kill everyone.

"A brown fog comes from the south to fill your lungs and cause a slow death. Before it nears the shore, all must enter tunnels underground. A hatch at a lone Elm on the northern side of a new reservoir needs protection. Find it in the low lands across the River where the meadows once grew before the Holoran Desert. I am leaving to build underground shelters for you with fresh air. Hide all Beaulancians inside and protect them. Use the new caverns for temporary quarters until the war is over. The caverns will hold every Beaulancian human or otherwise. Bring livestock and any wild creatures in need of rescue."

Captain Jessica Brodnick steps up, "I will personally see that this dispatch is followed by all, sir horse!"

She says to the Lieutenant, "Notify the regimen to prepare to evacuate."

Utopio says, "An exit will be found under your headquarters soon. Make a trapdoor large enough for twenty to enter at a time. Stock the caverns with water guns, food, medicine, blankets, clothes and toiletries. There will be another tunnel under where I stand. Make a hatch large enough for horses and livestock to enter. I will make the tunnel wide enough for twelve horses in a row and add storage rooms. Excess dirt will pile in mounds above ground as walls to shield you from attack." Do not worry about the native wild creatures that find shelter there within. Coexist with them during the fog."

Captain Brodnick says, "Look at the coming toxic haze on the horizon, Lieutenant. Do as he says. It will soon be upon us."

Utopio says, "The Blessing and irrigation ditches are polluted. Do not drink or eat fish or wash with the water. I provided fresh water in the shelters down under. Protect the reservoir with your lives. It is our best armament and resource."

He then puts his head down in humility hoping for a favorable reaction. The soldiers accept instructions but the Lieutenant asks,

"Why don't you show me?"

Utopio allows the Lieutenant to jump on his back bringing sense to his head. He flies him there in a non-dimensional second and back, lickiddy-split, and then asks,

"Want to see it again?"

The horrified Lieutenant shouts, "Captain, mam, Evil beings are on way to the salt dome with a wagon train of slaves. A caped villain leads them on my old Appaloosa!"

The Captain never obeyed the Commander in Chief's orders to stop battle preparedness. She ordered an oversupply of skins since the rescue mission in noticing the returning soldier's uncoordinated strange be-havior. She now orders troopers to gather armaments hurriedly. They salute the Captain and Utopio before dispersing. The wrangling Calvary collects a string of extra horses. They will enter the tunnel diverted to underground stables. Other soldiers begin loading furniture on big wag-ons for their dwellings underground. Nurses divide food, medicine, pil-lows, blankets, and books into sacks. Soldiers move to positions around the fort on lookout platforms to watch the city and fields until Utopio's shelter is ready. The army is adequately informed and armed.

Utopio swiftly leaves to check on Scout. He is so fast, before you real-ize he is gone he is already there, saying, "Scout, Scout, wake up!"

Scout asks, "Huh?"

Utopio nuzzles his side belly asking, "You okay?"

Scout answers, "Me tummy ache, feel pain inside, no mistake, like sour mash collide. Ewe, my belly bitter like turnip jelly, Ewe, my tummy blurts with hurts."

Utopio blows cloudy blue gas from his nostrils onto Scout's right-side-up stomach.

The pain is gone. He pauses with surprise and then rejoices shout-ing, "Scout up and about, I rhyme like in better time. I wave wings and fly to tout. Scout knows what it is all about! I fly down to watch the mess from a tree I sit and watch the rest. I am Scout, and will to Topio thank, for help, no doubt!"

Utopio jumps for joy, saying, "Eh, Whymmhinny, emhenny, enha, henniny, en, en, eh, en, ah, ennen, yenn, yna, heny, enha, wynnyhinn, ah, slobber, slobber! You are well again, Scout. You can fly high in the sky and stay out of sight. You will see what Evil does and tell us all about."

Scout says, "Yes, Scout will fly high."

Utopio says, "Bring intelligence to Spirit at Beaver Lake. Keep an eagle eye on the coast. I will be digging chambers for everyone under-ground. You will not see me for a while."

Scout says, "You go, Topio, go, go, go! I tell Spirit what I know. Away my wings do proudly spread. Above the Evils I am led."

He glides high into a windy blue yonder above clouds. Utopio dashes off the cliff and quickly disappears into a gully. Cain's party hacks fankdustles at cactus and whips slaves to move faster. Scout watches from high above through veiled clouds. Red puffs rapidly blink from volcanos on the coastal horizon. The platinum ship is slowly advancing from far out at sea with another delivery of hazardous waste.

Utopio is already under the elm tree creating a superhighway and jumbo subdivision for survivors. His white yellow and red snaking form carves out bedrooms, dining rooms, bathrooms, water troughs, birdbaths, hand pumps, valves, faucets, and drains. He blinks a wish for sanitary air filtering vents and they instantly appear everywhere. He blinks for food, water, and light and they bloom throughout a multitude of chambers. In only a few hours, the entire project is finished. He is a faithful and most capable servant from Folkhaven. The three well-trained celestial studs can do anything Strong Am wills.

⌒⧊⌒

I Bandy am Utopio's mentor but he follows his own intuition. Our power is as infinite as God wills and everlasting in our homeland. Spirit and Astro studied with me long before Topio. They have had my great admiration for many years. They are all family regardless of bloodlines. The havenly figures rejoice in seeing put to use their mighty gifts. Utopio's ancestry has forever chivalrously carried the greatest burdens in wars and we are of the same bloodlines. Before his time, I was born to go, to and fro', wherever needed or wanted. I live forever and with gratitude to my keepers for the righteous powers bestowed on me. Time has no effect on us havenly beings. We live forever in the primmest forms. Our generosity has no bounds. We rescue the defenseless and bring messages to those in the fold. This keeps us young forever. Wingless or not we have abundant powers against evil-minded attackers. I keep watch to warn and protect to the best of my ability.

Chapter 16

EVIL CRISIS

Cain is close to the salt dome on Stumble Hill Trail near the diamond back incident with Utopio. Hostages tied behind wagons drag along. A demon points up saying with a deep rumbling voice, "Look, Master, a flame passes below the sun!"

It is Utopio flying above. He spots them and the platinum ship on the horizon. Angelic telepathy tells him, Astro is standing in the hull and Molly is sitting on the floor, shackled to eyebolts on the bulkhead. Utopio dashes in the sky behind the wagon train. Cain sees the flash like a daytime shooting star and shouts, "My father is blotting the sky, spy! Your flight will soon be out of sight. You will never find us again. There is nothing, you can do about it, you little grunt, whoever you are, Uh-hahahahaha, Lava Clan, move your tails! Daddy hates tardiness!"

The beastly drivers lash the horses to pull buckboards faster with the hostages tied to a towrope at the rear. Adults and children drag behind, stumbling and moaning in pain. Five wagons roll along in double file and the captives succumb to tripping. The whip-snapping demons harass people to stay on foot. The dogs or gargies rant, growl and bark as they crisscross over and under the towlines to keep folks scared and moving over the rocky trail.

Utopio invisibly lands at Jake's place entering the tightly locked barn and immediately appears brightly visible passing through the wall inside.

Talking to the stable animals in a glowing, lighted form, he says, "Do not worry fellow creations. We intercede for Beauty- land. The next few days may see sorrow as anyone may give up life in sacrifice for the victory to come. A horror is about to unfold but do not despair. My family and I are preparing for victory and the attackers will perish. Life will be more wonderful than ever. Believe it wherever you happen to be. Soon all of the Evil intruders will become unworthy dust under your feet and safety you will have again. Allow what I say to keep you on guard for the retribution you deserve. When the noise settles and the air smells like roses, trumpets will sound. Come out from your given shelters and rejoice!"

He invisibly exits through the door again and visibly appears whinnying, a super siren in the open yard. Will guards the fence and Hank guards the well with each covering their ears. The barn-cooped animals scramble in the spontaneous noise. The amazing musical siren draws Jake, Max, Kristin, Takoda, and even the fully revitalized Judy to the deck of the front porch. Jake moves quickly down the stairs to the yard. He puts one hand on Utopio's smooth yellow fibrous nose and the other on his long soft red mane between his ears, saying, "Topio, I can't thank you enough for bringing Kristin back home. Have you any news to tell of the invaders whereabouts?"

Utopio answers, "I do and can tell you Cain's wagon train is towing humans and horses southwest of Salt Dome Caverns. The platinum ship is approaching the desert shore and Astro and Molly are aboard. Astro is protecting her. I came to warn you, the conflict is about to explode. There will be need for intervention with a deadly show of force against the invaders. If any are able to fight then prepare your water weapons. Be diligent and attack in numbers. A trap floor in your bedroom will lead you into a tunnel to the main shelters. The shelters have supplies enough to last the duration of our defense.

"When the southern sky turns brown, go underneath. Tunnels lead to the center of the city, the army headquarters, to the forests and under the Blessing. I have created a new reservoir near the desert. Fresh water plumbs throughout the caverns for ammunition and sustenance. The Evils know nothing of it. The army is on way to keep guard. Escape through the tunnel and you will have all that you need to survive. There are hatches under the barn, chicken coop, and pigpens. Let in all of your animals and all of the wild ones that may seek refuge. There are rooms and stalls for everyone. Charlie is in command at the port."

Jake and everyone steps back in awe of the details.

"How much time do we have?" he asks.

Topio replies, "Help is needed to stop Cain at the Salt Dome Caverns before Blaze arrives and takes control of the hostages! Whoever can go must ready and go!"

Jake answers, "I will be there!"

"I'm ready," says Will.

Hank insists, "I'm going!"

Ben answers, "Count on me!"

They set out to pack and Takoda leaves to warn his people. He will send braves to protect Judy and the kids. Utopio waits until everyone is gone and flies back to the port.

Charlie gave orders to turn raincoats into water guns and empty metal drums of soy sauce from China to make depth charges. They fill them with water, gunpowder and cannonballs, to explode under the platinum ship. A large barrage could sink it. Charlie keeps an eye out over the ocean from a lighthouse.

Utopio appears through a window floating with a large leather pouch strung over his neck. He whinnies and asks, "Admiral, how far is the platinum ship from the beach?"

Charlie puts a telescope to his eyes and answers, "It is close. They could dock by sundown. I am coming out to you on the balcony"

Utopio instructs, "Admiral, do not attack there. Your mission is to attack the Island of Relief. Load your vessels with quicklime and water by the barrelful. Add a tiny sprinkle of my ground hoof powder to every container. Fill cisterns and connect pumps and hoses to drench volcanoes through the reachable shaft hatches. Drop the drums into more distant hatches."

Charlie agrees, "I will do whatever you say! The city has many warehouses full of quicklime for making whitewash, mortar, paper, and limelight. Have all the people been warned?"

Utopio answers, "Yes and the army is gathering people into extensive underground shelters with limelight illumination under all of Beauty. The city streets will soon be empty. Migration is almost complete. Abandoned warehouses are available for seizure. Collect all the lime you can. Make enough water skins for every sailor. Many Lava Clans remain on the island. You must rescue enslaved mustangs and humans. Capture their wagon stockade. They carry enriched barrels to inland smokestacks. Grab your victory and return to Beautyland. Have faith, we horses of Grace are not far away!"

Utopio bends down and drops the pouch to the balcony into Charlie's hand.

Charlie salutes, saying, "Aye, aye, Utopio!"

He grabs a bullhorn off a hook beside the window and shouts, "Sailors, fall in!"

All work stops. Men and women gather on the docks looking up at the lighthouse balcony. He explains the mission. They form ranks and immediately begin assembly. Utopio disappears in the air to the desert coastal dock. He disguises as a pelican landing on a pylon at the outer edge of the pier waiting for the platinum ship.

Jake, Will, Ben, Hank, and the Private trot on the way to the salt dome. Saber Toes sees them nearing the spring from a cliff. Lucer with a face like a wolf guards the spring's entrance with gorisilles and other gargies. Saber Toes runs down meowing safely like a kitten and says, "Hey Ranger dudes stay away from the spring. The bad mambo wambos want trouble with you horsey dudes. It's better for you duty dudes to stay out of sight!"

Jake says, "Thanks Saber we will then. Come on Rangers we can cross the river upstream. Keep looking out Saber Toes. We will see you later."

They divert the area as guards eat phosphorus rocks unaware of the shrinking river. The Rangers cross the shallow riverbed to shrub land and up to the mesa above the cavern. Cain's party is at the entrance arguing about duties when Blaze arrives. Cain's horse rears trying to throw him off. The arguing intensifies about who will be the boss when his Daddy shows up. One gorisille looks at dead gargies dried out like pumice in the entrance and says,

"Someone has been here. Our guards are dead."

Cain sees the remains saying, "Cool it Thunder you stupid horse. What happened here? Stop jerking me around, Thunder, you stupid horse. Death to all celestial steeds, they are sure to blame." Four gorisilles raise multipurpose fankdustles as lances and reply "Life for Lava Clan. Death to celestial steeds," in their language.

Cain raises a lance saying, "Death to all Beautyland!"

The Rangers on the top of the mesa watch the drama until Jake signals everyone to fall back for a meeting. One hundred yards away he says, "I counted twenty-six demons, not including Cain, eight dogs, and thirty humans, including children. Save them and save that Appaloosa horse! It's a beaut!"

The Private says, "That was a cavalry horse traded in at the Plenty Good Stables. The Lieutenant never could control it. He is a four-year-old gelding and full of spirit. I know him. Fabian is his first given name."

Jake adds, "Great, I want him. Now, just how can we do this?"

Mumbles quietly overlap.

Ben adds, "I don't know?"

Jake insists, "I have an idea. We will spread out to the slopes on each side of the butte and charge down to surround them. Hank and the Private go to the right, Me, Will and Ben will go to the left. At the bottom spread out, drawing the demons attention, while I go straight after Cain! Do not look in their eyes or at their lances. Just shoot at anything too gruesome to save and try to cover me. Fight with fury and we will massacre them with these water guns. I'll capture that descendant from hell."

The Private adds, "I'll save Fabian for you."

Jake insists, "Whatever happens do not kill Cain. I want him alive!"

Will agrees, "You are right, Jake. We can do this but why spare Cain. We should kill him."

Jake answers; "His father is Blaze Evil, the brains for this outfit. He is on his way here. We can use Cain to draw Blaze into a trap and the salt dome has cells to hold him."

Will says, "OK!"

Jake asks, "Is everyone ready?"

They all answer, "Yes!"

The Rangers wildly charge down and swiftly drop to the road aiming water sacks nuzzled under arms. The hostages smile proudly seeing the rescuers. A colorful ruckus ensues with bluish water blasting against red lasers. Yellow acidic balls of brimstone launch from the flexible slinging ends of fankdustles. The splatter guns dilute the balls and kill several demons in the act. The remaining gorisilles fire lasers from versatile fankdustle tips. The Rangers block those with defusing sprays. The enemy quickly puts fankdustles to other use such as laser swords and heavy platinum clubs. The horses out maneuver their swings by cutting sharply and running. Every close encounter makes it easier for the Rangers to douse deadly water. The demons create a diversion going after captives to use as a barrier from blasts. They threaten injuring captives by firing brimstone at them.

Cain relishes heinous torture and screams, "Blind them!"

The targeted victims cry out in pain. One ball just misses Ben's head. Luckily, he ducked to the side of his horse just in time and it missed. He shoots a pistol cutting the towline in half and lets captives free. *Whoosh,* goes a ball by Hank's ear. He shoots the beast that fired it. He pulls a Colt .45 from a holster and fires five shots into the rope holding a string of horses. Ben grabs seven handguns from his four saddlebags and throws them on the ground, shouting, "Shoot your cuffs off!"

He and Ben each drop spare water guns and a medical pouch. Hank shouts, "Wash out your eyes and skin. Save some water to defend yourselves!"

Ben charges back to battle against a dog after Will. Jake keeps his head down away from Cain's hypnotic laser eyes and a flexible, electrified, fankdustle whip. The lash has a cup at the end like an octopus tentacle. It can paste brimstone dust balls to eyes with flame igniting voltage. Fortunately, Cain slashes like a damsel in distress or to say his coordination is amiss would be an understatement. He cannot hit a thing because he keeps his forearms to low when he swings. However, his eyes make a match to reckon with. If he catches anyone with those lasers or in a hypnotic stare, it would cause real trouble. The good thing is his fear of water keeps him away and his eyes are most powerful at close range. If not looked into they are harmless. Jake and the others stay carefully at a distance. Captives, including horses and wounded people have severed shackles for freedom.

The battle rages on as the water guns dilute stinging powder and defuse lasers in the air. Splashes hit Cain's electric whip and send shocks back to his hand. The Rangers are drenching beasts into smoldering tar. Hairy fingers just melt off fankdustles to the ground and only two gorisilles, Cain, and three scared gargie beasts remain. Hostages stay behind buckboards washing each other with water and rubbing alcohol for maximum relief. Will steers to fire at two attacking gargies. He hits one and it transforms into a smoking puddle. Ben blasts the other. The Rangers fight like polo playing athletes in dodging sulfur balls and searing lasers. They shoot long soaking streams at gorisilles and gargies almost to the point of elimination. Hank battles a fierce gorisille whose club almost knocks him out of the saddle when it hits his back. Will comes to the rescue and splashes it down.

Jake has no other choice than to hide behind an extension of the butte to keep away from Cain's repetitive electric fankdustle lashings. He needs help and so does Ben as his horse is frantically trying to rear. It bucks as the last beast alive has hold of its neck. Just in time, before the beast kills bens new horse, Will is there to blast it down. The horse is still scared and acting up. Control is one of the big problems in a battle like this, especially, on a new horse. Jake finally darts out from under cover and tosses a rope around Cain saying, "Mission accomplished!"

He tightens it around his arms at the abdomen and then reels slack around the saddle horn and puts a spit bubble bead on his water shooter-nozzle. He aims it directly between Cain's eyes. Fabian rears throwing Cain to the ground. Hank loops a rope over the horse and hands it to the Private. Will loops another rope around Cain and drags him to his belly. They all watch without looking directly at him. Jake keeping shooter pointed and head down shouts, "Get up!"

Cain rises to his feet with hot orange saliva slightly running out his mouth grumbling, "You can't keep me!"

Jake says, "Watch me!"

Ben races over to a buckboard and grabs good shackles for Cain's hands.

Jake remarks, "Try anything stupid and your dead. We won't think twice about it. Some us would prefer you would and I might anyway! If you want to live then hang on."

Jake holds the ropes attached to Cain and kicks his horse into a gallop yelling, "Yeehaw, monster man. It is true what they say. You are a drag!"

He drags Cain over old dead beasts through the entrance to deep inside the salt dome. Some lanterns still burning light the way. He comes to a dead stop at the downed stable gate. Hank follows but loses them in a dark corridor until turning sharply left into a lit hall and finds them at the end. Cain lies exhausted on his belly with a red-hot face.

Hank dismounts explaining, "The others are helping the hostages. What do we do with him?"

Jake pulls Cain over the broken gate. A well-built stall in the back looks secure. Blaze had it made for Black Rain. It is complete with a gate and padlock dangling from a steel loop. He dismounts, lifts Cain to his feet, pulls him inside, closes the gate, slides the bolt and pad locks it. Only Blaze has the key. Jake aims the water gun saying, "Make any funny moves and have a wet day in hell!"

Cain slips his rump down the far salty wall saying, "My father prepares hell for you!"

Jake instructs, "Hank, bring the shovels. We'll dig a wide shallow moat in front of the cell. It has to be too big to jump across."

Hank goes to his horse at the gate and brings back two small folding camp shovels. They dig the trench and pour ten gallons of water from spare guns.

"We should nail a skin to the wooden frame above the door and make a booby trap, just to be safe," says Hank.

Jake agrees, "Good idea."

Hank hammers two ten penny nails with the butt of a .45 and attaches a water skin. Jake fastens a leather trip string around the sack to the gate saying,

"There he sits. The slightest tension will cause it to discharge. The nozzle points perfectly at him. It will spray hard and wide. It can't miss."

"Let me test it," Hank says in jest.

Jake ties the drag rope around Cain's arms as leash to the gate and asks, "Who feels threatened now?"

Cain mumbles, "It's not over," and very carefully sits back against the wall. He shifts his cape off his shoulders and taps a platinum belt buckle with an index finger. They avoid looking at his eyes or wavy pinstripe shirt. His pants wore a hole when dragged and he has a fiery-red leg abrasion. Reflections from his platinum boot tips and vest buttons glimmer on the inside walls. The experienced men only use peripheral vision. Cain's black and red hair hangs down covering his cheeks as he whispers in an evil and eerie, childlike way, "Daddy's coming!"

Spirit lands outside the salt dome surmising the situation. Ben, Will, the Private and freed folks run up to greet him.

Spirit whinnies loud and responds, "You finished an excellent skirmish here!"

Ben replies, "Yep, we did and Jake trapped Cain inside there as bait for Blaze. All of the other wicked varmints are dead."

Spirit warns, "Pick up dead demons and fankdustles. Load them on buckboards and dump the evidence in an out of sight gulley. By the way, I have great news! How is your water holding out?"

"Well, we used quite a bit in this struggle," says Will!

Spirit asks, "Have you heard about the new reservoir? It is not far from here."

Ben replies, "Yes, Utopio told us."

Spirit adds, "I saw him only moments ago posing incognito at the coast. Blaze will arrive at the old cattle merchants dock soon with a big army. You are all going to follow me to the reservoir. Soldiers there are guarding it and will lead you safely through a secret hatch to a fantastic underground shelter."

Ben asks, "How long will it take us to get there and back again?"

Spirit insists, "No more than four hours one way. You will not be coming back."

Will replies, "We must come back to hold Cain and fight off his father."

Spirit answers, "You cannot win that battle. He is too strong.

Jake and Hank hear the conversation from inside the cavern. They speed up exiting and greet Spirit obstinately.

Jake insists, "Hank and I are staying put. Cain must be guarded."

Spirit argues, "No, sir! All of you must leave and stay gone. My mouth will syphon water from the reservoir and flood the caverns. I promise it will keep the jack-a-dandy from escaping. You Jake will take charge of another major conflict to occur elsewhere.

We steeds can survive the coming putrid fumes and brimstone but you cannot. Stay underground in the tunnels preparing for the right time. You will fight the big one on a much larger scale, I promise. Keep your weapons loaded an intuition for preparedness will come. The big battle over Beauty is drawing near. The beavers and I are still working on the Dam to dry out the river. It will hold and protect the environment. We installed a cover over Beaver Lake. If the fallout reaches far north, it will not penetrate the water. Fret not great Rangers! Soon your time will come. We Folkhaven steeds have preparations underway. Until you have the necessary survival equipment, stay underground! Everyone should help clean up this battlefield and afterwards follow me. I will float above to watch the coast for my brother returning on the ship. I will lead you safely through the desert to the reservoir. Heed what I say. This is not a test."

He boldly lifts waiting the finished cleanup and never looking so super.

Chapter 17

RETURNING TO DESTROY

Used-up animals and humans from the Island return to Beautyland to haul the last weapons of mass destruction to Salt Dome Caverns. Deadly Sulfur Dioxide plumes, spew from smokestacks over the ocean behind the platinum ship. Astro rests in the hold with Molly, Colima, and other mustangs and human slaves. Thousands of angry gargie jackals and many more demons fill the decks, ready for war. The ship reeks with smells of rotten food and creature extrusions. Breathing is sensory torture and the journey drags on fighting hunger. The food on board is rancid. After sunset, a loathsome crew prepares landing stations, and Blaze saddles Black Rain on the main deck.

Astro bides his time like everyone else until the ship approaches the dock. It remains a long way off on the dark horizon. The moon is full and the ocean is calm. Colima lies in filth, snorting with a bloated stomach.

"Help me Astry," she pleads.

He pushes between crowds and scoots over saying, "I am here, Colima. Touch my coat and you will be healed."

She sticks her nose up until it touches his and feels an amazing cure. She shakes with goose bumps, rises and says, "Oh, Astro, I feel great. I am not even hungry."

Astro replies, "And you look great too, uh-huh, uh-huh!"

Colima stretches the slack in the rope around her neck and moves closer to him. His eyes gaze intensely at hers. She smiles back with wide-eyes blinking and nuzzles her nose to his cheek saying, "Astry baby, I am not hungry anymore. How did you fix that?"

He answers, "Uhh, well, I guess you are not the first to lose an appetite over me."

She asks sultrily, "Where are you going when you finish here, big boy?"

Astro moves his eyes away from her lovely presence and shyly says, "Uhh well, I am going home, I guess."

"Where is home?" she asks.

Astro says, "Home sweet home, ah, huh, yes, home, my pretty Lima, is through the sky, farther away than sees your eye and home is here with you, but where my family is too!"

Colima asks, "Could I meet them?"

With a lump in his throat, he stutters, "Uhh, of course, U-u-topio and Spir-ir-it sure you can."

She says, "Oh good I cannot wait to meet your brother and your cousin too."

A knocking from the floor above rustles all hostages to attention as the ship slows down close to shore.

Although exhausted and starving, Molly stands to her feet and says, "Get ready! The ship is going to dock. They're preparing anchor."

Utopio perched on a pylon at the end of the pier watches as a pelican. He sees Blaze on the main deck atop Black Rain, ready to come ashore. Two bred and trained dragon lizards guard the horse's stance. Another two Gorisille beasts cast mooring lines to two others on the pier who wrap them around dock cleats. Then another beast winds a crank lowering a ramp to the dock. Blaze rides down it dominantly clad in black almost invisible in the darkness of early morning. His two lizard friends follow wobbling in a run. They're the size of Komodo dragons but much worse in temperament and can spit fire off their mutant reptilian tongues.

Blaze wears his long cape and bandit-style hat as he sits atop the large and strong evil black warhorse and plunges his spurs into its sides. Black Rain rears high. His nostrils spew amber puffs and periwinkle foam flows over the bit and out his mouth. He bolts down the pier toward the beach. Utopio flies above Blaze and knocks his hat off with his metamorphosed pelican beak. He then pokes each of the lizards sharply enough to puncture their thick skin and carries their carcasses out to the sea like on a skewer and drops them dead in the water. He whispers, "No breeding allowed." Black Rain sees a trace of an illusionary aurora highlighting the shape of a horse as Utopio returns. The vision puts him in a spirited frenzy. He rears, performs a sharp about-face and throws Blaze onto the dock. He points his nose to direct Blaze's attention.

Utopio flies to the ship's crow's nest. Blaze's eyes look for a pelican, but faster than he can catch sight, Topio changes into a seagull and flies to a flock circling above the stern. The bald marauder picks up his hat, stands and raises his fist shouting, "I will smack you to dust whoever you are. Just try that again, you coward!"

The seagulls laugh like hyenas around the ship's stack. Blaze shoots vengeful twin red lasers from his eyes at them. A wave crashes over the pier, throws him off balance, and he misses. He hits a smokestack on the platinum ship instead and the gulls disappear behind it. Topio as a seagull swoops down to a guardrail above a large open elevator shaft. He hears beasts below gather captives. Astro, Colima, and Molly stick together. The scary demons squeeze about forty mustangs at a time onto a platform below the shaft. Colima and Astro hide Molly between them during shoving. The lift fills up with mustangs. One demon pulls a rope, and the floor rises to the main deck. At the top, more hairy monsters move them off using weapon-grade prodding staffs and hitch them to buckboards full of poisonous arsenals.

Astro and Colima luckily hitch together on the same covered wagon. Molly sneaks from underneath Astro. She goes below the chassis, climbs in the back, and hides in a cranny between barrels of chemical compounds. Drivers move them and many other supply wagons off the ship, as more captives are loaded from the hull into the returned elevator. They roll their loads of toxic materials down the ramp to the dock all the way to the corral on the beach. Blaze waits there and directs them inside. As the corral fills, he aligns the excess in double file along the shore.

Next, unshackled sick people, almost crawling to exit the ship, make their way to available spots on the beach and collapse. Six hours pass during the unloading process. The multitudes of various beings on the shore conceal the sand. The sun will rise in two hours. Inside the crowded corral, Molly crawls through the wagon silently behind the demon in the driver's seat. She grabs him around the throat. Astro and Colima feel the struggle. The demon suddenly gasps for air and murmurs, "uh!"

The horses give no reaction knowing what is happening. They maintain poise among other wagons and the surrounding beasts. Her perspiring hands save her from the challenge of choking him to death. He goes limp. She pulls him backward into the covered wagon. His neck smolders to the brain. Molly removes his dog leather overalls to wear on the driver's seat over her plaid shirt with his hat low over her face and grabs the reins. Astro looks back and winks.

Neither the corral nor the beach is big enough to hold all captives. Blaze no longer needs so many. He sets the useless ones free to climb the palisades. He gets attention with a thunderous crack of the whip saying, "All humans and unbridled mustangs may leave now. You are free, *hehheh, hahaha*. Try to reach Plentyville alive. I give you your freedom. Go ahead and chance my coming doom on your beloved land! Go now before I change my mind!"

Snap goes the whip again, "Get lost," he says.

In weak health, this new freedom motivates the emancipated group up a coyote path on a cliff off the Holoran desert. Blaze cracks more lashes directing thousands of gorisilles (gore-a-sills) and gargies into motion, shouting, "Move out before I blister all of you. Get into single file up the road behind the warehouse. Hurry up! Move it!"

He holds back some gargies and gorisilles to direct a speedy convoy off the beach. Backed-up wagons begin flowing up around the warehouse. The corral empties last. Molly's wagon falls in at the rear. Blaze rides behind her shouting, "Faster, faster all the way you slowpokes! Where is that stupid son of mine? He should be here by now. Where are the replacements? We need fresh horses."

Just then, an extra ugly, furry, red, demon sergeant, slobbering over his beard with slurred speech, through missing front teeth, asks, "Should I send Taslas to find him?"

Taslas is a very large demon. He can jump bushes twelve feet high and across ditches thirty feet wide. He must be at least ten feet tall and eight hundred pounds of pure muscle besides his bushel basket size head.

Blaze says, "I said send Taslas!"

The ugly sergeant says, "Of course you did, right away, your majesty."

He races back down the road to get him and at the ship he screams, "Taslas, where are you?"

He finds him drunk on fermented mustang urine lying wasted on his back next to a portable moonshine still in the empty hull. The red sergeant swats a lance saying, "Get up, you retard,"

Taslas rubs his stung thigh, turns over on all fours, and crawls onto the elevator. The sergeant pulls the rope, bringing the platform down. He drags the drunkard on and pulls the rope again to go up. At the main deck, he kicks Taslas in the shins shouting, "Get out!"

Go find Evil's son!"

Taslas rises towering over the Sergeant. He steps off the platform wavering for the ramp. After only four, six-foot long lazy stretches, he trips on the ramps lip and rolls groggily down, sixty feet to the pier and overboard. He tussles in the water unable to swim or touch bottom. His huge splashing body quickly reduces to reddish steaming surface ooze in the salty crashing waves. The wind spreads embers above the surf. He shrinks to only a bobbing head and grumbles with his last breath,

"I'm garble, garble, dead drunk," and disintegrates into a washed-out ball of fur on the beach.

Blaze bolts on Black Rain to the pier and over loose lifting planks to the end. He forces the stunned sergeant aside shouting histrionically, "What is happening here? The Sargent answers, "Taslas fell in the surf and disintegrated."

Blaze understands, "Oh, I get it, he, he, ho, ho! The Pelican did it. You think you are slowing me down, don't you, Pelican?"

Utopio replies, "Squawk!"

His Aura illuminates in threatening agreement. Blaze looks up to find the squawker but flocks of screeching seagulls block his view.

He says, "I know you had something to do with this, pelican. I will get you! From dust to mush you will be mine. My fist rises to squish you with bare hands. You will never taste a fish again. You are doomed!"

He is unaware Utopio is a seagull and no longer a pelican. Black Rain however, saw the change and aims twin red beams at the flock. Blaze watches the beams and is about to get a glimpse when Black Rain goes into a conniption fit. Utopio is taunting his hooves with yellow beams. He whinnies and rears in a sharp turn to follow the flock to the piers end and slides to a stop nearly throwing Blaze into the brink. Blaze is oblivious and only holding on during the thrill ride.

Utopio dives into the water behind the ship as a porpoise swimming toward the Port of Beauty. He pops out around a corner past the palisades and dives down again deeper. A great blue whale watches with delight as Utopio transforms back into himself and trots out onto a deserted beach. He faces the waves whispering to the whale, "It won't be long!"

He rises in the air over the desert and finds the emancipated slaves scavenging for food in the new day's sun. He swiftly floats down to hover whinnying and says, "Gather round me, one and all. Follow me and I will lead you to shelter, food and water. His gravity-less mobility shocks them with unbelief and the fear of more tricks lying ahead. It sounds too good to be true. An aged pinto looks up saying, "Your colors differ but you resemble another horse angel named Astro."

Topio explains, "He is my cousin. I have come to help! Where is he now?"

The gray replies, "Harnessed to a wagon the last time I saw him."

A weary chestnut mare mentions, "He is pulling a load of poison to Salt Mine Caverns."

A black mare adds, "Nothin' doesn't never seem to bother, that colorful stallion. Even when whipped, he doesn't flinch!"

A frail old man standing next to his exhausted wife says, "I've seen the pony put on a good act. He is a smart one to turn heads."

The whole crowd smiles in agreement.

Utopio explains, "Astro never loses a good attitude. I will catch up with him after all of you are safe."

An elderly man takes hands off sore bent knees stretching tall saying, "If you have come to take me, then take me now. I am ready to go."

Others shout, "Take me. Take me. Take us all!"

Topio turns toward the reservoir and back to look over the hundred plus dehydrated humans and mustangs barely stumbling along. He slowly leads them with a protective shadow casted over the hot trail. Clear blue water suddenly appears and it is not a mirage. Topio lands at the reservoir pointing ears to the Elm on the rise saying, "There stand soldiers waiting to guide you to underground sanctuary. Go and do not be afraid. Rancid air with acidic yellow flakes will soon fall from the sky. Only we celestial steeds can survive it. Have no fear. I led you in truth. Stay underground until you hear the trumpet of triumph signal victory!"

Back on the trail, Astro bit through his harness and is biting off Colima's. A brigade of Lava Clan is marching behind in columns. Black Rain is prancing mightily for Blaze at the rear. Another battalion leads the caravan. The wagonloads foul air with rotten smells and draw deep-ruts in the road as they progress.

Astro's fibrous coat begins glowing blue and yellow like the sky camouflaging their every move. His tail spreads out keeping Colima concealed as he turns around covering Molly with his mane. She jumps to his back unseen in the illusion. He tightly wraps strands around both and lifts abruptly off the ground. They leave unnoticed as the wagon slows dragging harnesses and tug chains. They glide away blending into clouds.

Blaze shouts from the rear to the vacant wagon, "What's your hold up? Stop picking your nose and keep going you good for nothing hoofers, I'll whip your hides off!"

He rides up finding empty hitches, stares in disbelief and shouts, "Where in Blazes are the horses? Where is the driver for cryin' shame? I am about to kill all of you good for nothings. Am I seeing things? What is happening here? How come no one told me they left?"

He casts the whip around a slouching gargie and lifts it with a powerful flick of his wrist to Black Rain's neck saying, "Tell me what went on here. Where are the team and driver?"

The hound yelps, "I don't know, errurrrp," as Blaze tightens the grasp.

"How can you not know, weren't you here all the time? What did you do? Did you go behind a bush or something while they got away?" he asks.

"No, your majesty, I've been keeping up. I have been in the same place behind the wagon all along," he says.

Blaze says, "Do you want to be choked to death? Tell me once more you saw nothing and I will kill you. Do you expect me to believe they just disappeared?"

The gargie whimpers, "Yes, your highness, I mean, no, no, no, you're heinous."

Blaze swirls the gargie by whip releasing him to a large pear-leaf cactus and asks, "Anyone else see what happened here?"

He rouses everyone near with lashes but none saw anything.

"Hitch this wagon and get it going before I beat you all to pumice," he shouts.

The driver in front explains, "But, your highness, we have no extra mustangs. You set them free."

Blaze says, "I want two gorisilles hitched right now! Where is my weaseling son and the replacements? Why isn't he here?"

He shakes his head in disbelief and kicks Black Rain into a run to the front shouting, "Whip, these miserable mustangs and hurry up. We're losing time!"

Astro sees Utopio at the lake and comes down. He loosens Colima to rest surely on the ground and Molly slides off his back. Utopio nuzzles him saying, "Astro, you are all right!"

He answers, "I am fine cousin but some adventure it has been. I'd like you to meet Colima, and of course you remember Molly!"

Utopio responds, "Eynineh, of course Molly our Goodman friend. Do not worry you are safe now. Has Astro taken good care of you? You look a little less for wear"

Molly remarks, "I am hungry and weak. At times, I thought I would drop. Astro kept me on my toes. I will never forget it."

"Don't think twice, it's my job and pleasure to help, 'em, hmm, yeah," says Astro.

Utopio addresses Colima, "And how do you do, fair mare?"

She curtsies in awe at his handsomeness and blushes by her own shambled appearance, saying, "Oh, I am fine, your steed/ship, thanks to Astro. His happy song gave me other things to think. They may have shriveled my lime but I simply could not have survived the horror alone!"

Topio adds, "And it is . . . hmm . . . a very pretty lime. I can see how that should be protected."

Astry shakes his head, bewildered by their communication, and sputters, "Not so fast, I saw her first."

She explains, facing Astro, "I was a very spoiled mare whose capture in the dark scared me beyond my normally contented spirit. They came and destroyed everything I had ever known and loved. They burnt down my stable and killed the caretakers. You made me feel safe again. Astro, I will be forever grateful."

He grins like winning the Triple Crown with a watermelon for a prize.

Colima says, "Ames told me so many great things about you, 'the magnificent Utopio,' he always said you were and you truly are! I have been so anxious to meet you. Now here I am. I couldn't be happier!"

Just then, all heads turn as Spirit rushes down from space.

Astro asks, "How are you, my brother? Look, I have brought back Molly."

Spirit bends his front legs before her, saying, "Good to see you looking so well."

Molly responds, "I am better than would be, thanks to your wonderful brother. I must say you look mighty fit since the last time I saw you. That was some studley landing, sir horse."

Spirit replies, "I am in excellent form. Never allow a first horse impression to fool you."

Astro interrupts, "Meet my friend, Colima. She is the 'lime in the coconut.' I met her in the ship's hull on the way to the island. We became close friends, and she wanted to meet you. I am pleased to introduce her!"

Spirit adds, "And I to meet her! It is a pleasure, Colima. I see you actually have an unusual lime situated there. This I guess means you are the coconut huh Astro hahaha!"

Astro replies, "Yeah right, you hear him, Colima. I am not the only comedian in the family."

Utopio says, "All right, everyone, the reunion will have to wait. Go Molly and lead Colima to the soldiers at the shelter. Stay there and wait for victory."

Everyone is in and the soldiers shut the hatch. The three studs fly to the far end of the lake and pull a hidden slate cover closed. The reservoir is now secure.

Chapter 18

A VENGEANCE

The destructive supply train reaches the caverns. Lucer, meets it with an evil barking pack, "Gruff, gruff, gruff, gruff, gruff," he says.

Blaze answers, "What are you doing here? Can't you follow orders? I told you to guard the spring."

Lucer prepares his voice with a gulp and says, "Masta, uh, the spring no more flows. The river not river, my lord, not even a stream. Eerrf, your heinous, eerrf, gulp, poison will not drift, Masta. What can we do?"

Blaze dismounts, repeating the question, "What can you do? How did you let this happen in the first place? Why has the spring suddenly, after eons, shut off?"

He kicks Lucer in the belly with a platinum-tipped boot and puts him on his back.

Lucer grunts, "Ouch, I do not know, you're heinous! It just shut off for no reason."

Blaze asks, "How in the world?"

Lucer cries, "I don't know, I don't know, arf, arf."

Blaze says, "Get up you wicked dog so I can kick you down again!"

Lucer is too sore to move.

Blaze says, "Take half of the gargie army, and search the area for clues. And you Sergeant Red, come here on the jiffy!"

Red runs up on furry red feet, saying, "Yes, your majesty, at your service. What would your majesty have me do?"

Blaze says, "Put your ear on that hole and listen."

Red climbs an incline beside the flooded entrance. He leans on the orifice pausing, listening and saying, "I hear humming!"

"What kind of humming," asks Blaze?

"A song your lordship!" says Red.

"What's the tune, stupid?" asks Blaze.

"Wait! I hear, do, do, do, sittin' in a salt dome! Sittin' down, down, down, down in a salt dome. Soon goin', gone, gone, gone, gone in a salt dome! It's no kinda fun, what happened to the fun! I am down, down, down, down in a salt dome!"

Red snapped fingers as he sung it back. Junior sings steadily and carefully as he sits.

Blaze shouts, "Move out of my way!" and takes over the spot.

He listens but hears nothing other than hydrosonic pulsations bouncing off cavern walls.

"Get out of here! You did not hear a thing! Whom do you think you are fooling? I demote you. You are a blaze red corporal again. Go back to your platoon!" he orders.

Then suddenly Cain's voice comes through clearly in a childish tone asking, "Daddy is that you?"

Blaze says, "Let me at that hole again. Move over, Corporal. So it is you, Junior? I should have guessed. Where have you been? Why didn't you deliver the wagons, fresh horses and slaves? What are you still doing in there? The warehouse is full and so is the cavern. Now everything in here is ruined. It's all wet. We can't touch anything. Junior, where are you? How is it still dry where you are? The whole cavern is flooded. Where did all this water come from? How many chambers are damaged?"

Junior answers, "Daddy, I am in Black Rains' stall facing a water gun pointed at my heart. Beaulancian Rangers attacked us and trapped me in here. Then water rushed in and stopped in front of the stall! I do not know how! They tied me to a booby trap! If I move, the gun will squirt me dead! I cannot move!"

Blaze asks, "Where are your cohort gorisilles?"

"They are already dead. Can't you see them laying on the ground out there?"

Blaze says, "No! There is nothing here but us. The ground does look burned though. I will try to get you out. Don't move."

"Right, don't worry, I won't move!" he answers.

Blaze cases the butte to a slope around the bend and finds what may be the opposite side of the stall and calls to Red, "Bring shovels and picks and dig here."

Red recruits five other gorisilles for the digging and supervises sitting on the ground while picking bugs off his shoulder.

Cain shouts, "I see sunlight shining on the wall. Is that you, Daddy?"

Blaze answers, "Yes, we are almost there. Keep still until the hole is big enough. Red will come in to let you loose. Red, can you see him yet?"

Red looks into the tunnel with big furry red mitts braced on his knees saying, "It's too narrow I am blocking the light. Dig out wider you hot bellies."

Cain shouts, "Be careful! You have to enter without rocking me. You are two feet away. The wall is cracking. Chunks are falling inside. Watch it you goonies,"

The hole finally expanded large enough to enter. Blaze crawls through to size up the situation, saying, "Well, dip-pity-ditz, now I know how to sit you still!"

Cain replies, "Daddy, you crawled through first? This is a big surprise. Do not start ragging on me now. Could you please this once? I thought we had them beat! They developed water guns! Can you see the sack above the gate? It fires powerful water spears. If I move, I'm dead so get me out of here real easy like, OK!"

Blaze angrily asks, "How did they know we were susceptible to water?"

Cain asks, "How do I know, maybe because they baptize with it? What do you think? Don't ask me. Just get me out of here!"

Blaze remarks, "You stupid Islander. I'll bet you gave them the idea dancing and squirming over a puddle like a little girl."

Cain insists, "No Daddy, we crossed over our buckboards and even one of their regular bridges. None of us ever came close to stepping in a puddle, let alone dancing over one!"

Blaze suggests, "Aha! Someone must have watched you! I bet it was the mangy pelican!"

Cain asks, "What pelican? There was no pelican where I was! Just get me out of here!"

In anger, his bound hand jerks and an accelerated squirt blasts with accuracy. Blaze pulls back just in time. A splash almost caught him.

"Oh! No! Cain, Cain!" he cries.

He cannot look again. The viewing end is damp. He listens to Cain's filthy crusty flesh disintegrate crackling and backs out crawling onto the sloped land shouting up at the mesa, "You got my son but you'll never get me! I am going to destroy Beautyland slow and painfully. Hear me Beautyland you are doomed! I will not let up. Suffer, Beauty! Suffer! This land is my land. No matter how bad I was, I am even worse now! I do not need my son's help to possess this land. I lost it once but never again! This land is mine. You got my son but you will not withstand me. I will defeat you. I am Evil. I am Blaze Evil! Red, prepare everyone to march."

Lucer returns explaining, "We found nothing, sire!"

Blaze orders, "Charge half the doggies down the western trail and kill anything and everything viciously. Be gone! To the rest of you this is destruction plan number one. Are you ready, demons?"

They answer, "We are, your majesty!"

Blaze commands, "Move out! Wagons hoe!"

Blaze gallops ahead toward the river.

Utopio says, "I have an idea," and leaves immediately without another word. Spirit and Astro look at each other and at the coming brown sulfuric haboob rolling in over the ocean.

Before Spirit zooms on to the reservoir, he shouts, "Get ready."

He did not next exclaim, "Set, go."

Astro looks disgruntled chasing up next to him. Lucer's pack of gargies snorts out flamethrowers to destroy the desert fauna with fire.

Lucer commands, "Grr- ruff, surround the reservoir."

Some sniff below the tree at the hatch. It is impossible for them to break in. He orders the others to sit silently around the reservoir facing him at the elm with no further instructions.

Chapter 19

THE RAVEN

The predicament gets dull for Astro. He asks, "What do you think? Should we make a move?"

Spirit insists, "Wait until dark. We are going to have some fun with those glowing embers in the smog. We can bury them in ash, my brother."

Astro replies, "But the ash will not hurt them."

Spirit adds, "I know it will blanket them from the cold desert night, my brother. You will sing a lullaby, put them to sleep and we can go check on Blaze."

"Wow, great idea elder brother, any requests for the show?"

"Just wait until night," Spirit exclaims!

Two hours pass and the fog rolls in. Flakes of yellow Sulfur Dioxide drop in a fiery mist of embers. Deadly chemicals fall and the air suddenly stinks. A normal nostril would burn and bleed, but the horses feel no pain. Nevertheless, the smell is nauseating.

Spirit instructs, "Attach your tail to mine and swing it like a jump rope. We will churn the fallout into a blanket."

"Right," Astro agrees.

He turns his rear and their tails interlock stretching over the lake, twirling, super-fast. Fallout gradually builds over the dogs. Their-weathered eyes close as Astro sings, "I hear the noises when I am dreaming. No more sighing, no more treaded over by the stalwart one! Lay my hairy head to your chest and I will comfort you. No more treaded over by the stalwart one, do not sigh no more. Live on Beautyland. Live on! I will always remember the days of island tremors. Live on Beauty. Live on. No more sighing, no more treaded over by the stalwart one. I hear the noises when I am dreaming. There will be peace when we are done"

Spirit remarks, "It worked, all the pit bulls are out like a light, unravel your tail and let us go."

They zoom fast ahead of slow scummy fallout to the spring where it meets the river. Astro catches a glimpse of Scout perched on a branch growing out of a crag adjacent to the river. He sits high watching the few remaining guards walk in and out of the cave. They come down to greet him with concern.

Spirit asks, "What are you doing here?"

"Checking out what is all about, messy air not yet here," squawks Scout.

Astro replies, "You are supposed to be underground like a gopher in a mound. The sky is changing. We have to do some rearranging."

"Know of hole in ground. Want to fly feathers before coming weathers. Happy I am outside not to hide unfound," says Scout.

Spirit replies, "Scout, you go into the shelter."

"Squawk, no. I stay, not afraid of yellow pew, watch from mountains away without dew," says Scout.

"He truly knows what it is all about. Maybe he will see news to benefit our doubt. He could inform between what's seen," advises Astro.

Spirit says, "The night is darkening. Stinky clouds with noxious fumes are swirling past the reservoir this way. Scout, if you will not go underground then go to Beaver Lake. The air should be safe there, alright?"

Scout answers, "Squawk, I will take the news job and for youse two's, will hob nob."

He flies slightly off course to the northwest.

Blaze reaches the River with thousands of demons and means of destruction. A little bugler boy gorisille called a gorl sounds an alert in the dark of night to the spring guards.

Blaze tells Red, "Unharness eight buckboards at the bank and unload. Remove the backboards and save them for connections. Roll the buckboards across as a bridge."

Red responds, "Yes you're heinous! Right away and if anyone slouches, I will throw him in the river."

He picks out the largest fifty gorisilles and lines them up along the trail beside the convoy. One big furry creature volunteers claiming, "I am the mightiest bruiser here for your service, sir."

Red accepts and turns to another, asking, "What about you, Muscles? Are you strong enough? I need thirteen troopers and have only twelve more to find. Can you unload a buckboard?"

"Yes, sir, I unload and reload."

"Get going then," says Red.

He points to a tall, wide monster, down the line, saying,

"Come over here, Brutus. I bet you could align the bridge all by yourself. Get on it."

He stands eight feet tall and shakes the ground walking. Red stumbles off trail into a Sycamore near the water's edge but quickly sturdies himself. At the top of the tree sits a very black raven watching everything. Red climbs back up to pick out the remaining ten strongest. They commence to unload the eight buckboards while Red sits comfortably watching from the riverbank. He catches a timid water moccasin curled in the grass and nibbles its head off. He drinks the venom and spits out the skull as if a popcorn seed.

Blaze cracks the whip, shouting, "Pick up the buckboard and place it across the river, you lanky gorl."

Brutus grabs it with both hands and lunges it across but slips off the bank. The shallow riverbed is still deep enough to kill. He is wet and disintegrates while clutching the rails. His hide shrinks to a blanket atop the stream and floats away. Blaze lifts his hat at the cliffs on the other side swearing, "I know you had something to do with this, pelican. Laugh now, but I will get you."

Black Rain raises an eyebrow in surprise seeing no pelican or imitation. Blaze seriously looks the place over. Red shoves two gorisilles behind another buckboard. His temper flares to get it set behind the other. He says, "Faster, everyone, get busy, make it happen or have some more of what Brutus got!"

Soon only one buckboard remains to finish the bridge. They use baling wire to connect the backboards as ramps. Blaze rides over first and up a hill on the other side. He dismounts and enters the cave to the spring. The gorisilles carry unloaded cargo across by hand. Red shoes away-unharnessed mustangs from the ramp to walk across. Some monsters fall off by shoving matches before reaching the other side and never get up again.

Hitched horses pull the wagons across into a dry ravine on the opposite bank. This is the end of the line for them. Starvation and labor has weakened them to the point of no return. Their spirits leave bodies one by one in the now bad air. Blaze comes out of the cave and the raven flies to the top of the mound to have a look. Blaze calls him to sit on a shoulder. His powerful suggestion is unavoidable for the bird.

Astro and Spirit see everything from an overhead cloud and Astro whispers, "Everything Blaze does leads to death."

Spirit replies, "For those unlucky enough to be on the same path it does."

Astro says, "He thinks he is so smart with a careless heart full of Beaulancian envy."

Spirit explains, "He drew a ticket to his own last breath this time! We will not wait any longer!

They zoom away in rarely displayed anger north toward Beaver Dam. The raven hits it off well with Blaze. He thinks it is not a problem for himself with the poisonous air. He is used to decomposing smells and rather enjoys it. They laugh about that because Blaze does too but promises Sulfur Dioxide and Carbon Monoxide will eventually kill him unless he strikes a deal.

The raven asks, "How can you save me?"

Blaze cuts a piece of his cape and says, "Take this and chew it."

The raven does and Blaze says, "Now swallow! When your stomach pooches, you will a have a little warm piece of me inside. I will guide you to everlasting life."

The raven burps, and a puff of orange smoke blows out. He quietly places a wing over his tail and puffs again. He utterly says,

"Hey! Wait a minute! This is not agreeable to me," and jumps off the shoulder back to the mound.

Blaze explains, "The deal was to save your life. We said nothing about how. I will save you from inside out. Obey, and we will live as long last friends. Do not worry, little me. I will keep you, *hehhehhehhahhahhah* alive!"

The raven replies, "No, no, I will poop you out."

Blaze remarks, "You have to find me first. I am nowhere close to where you feel worst, *ehhehhehhah!* Now I want you to go and kill the pelican. Return with his head and I will set you free!"

The raven flaps in lift to the forest, asking, "Pelican, pelican, where would a pelican be?"

He stops on a Juniper around the bend to think this through when suddenly his stomach hurts with a knock from little Blaze. He lifts off again heading for the coast.

Chapter 20

SCOUT, INDIANS, AND THE SUPERNATURAL

Scout soars over hills in Indian land under a full moon. He surprisingly spots many tribes in the night banded together on horseback. They wear full wardress with war-painted horses and heavy buffalo-hide water blasters over shoulders. Jake, Will, Hank, Ben, Molly, Judy, Kristin, and Max, with Lady at his side are going to meet the Indians on the forested plateau. Takoda rides a white, black-spotted Appaloosa beside his father, Chief Wiseoda. The Chief rides a tall white, pink-eyed Indian pony. His long feather headdress waves in the breeze.

They trot far ahead of the tribes to Goodman's militia. Jake is on a sorrel ranch horse. Will is on a bay with a white strip face, and Ben rides a black-and-white Tobiano paint. Hank is on a dapple blue roan; Molly rides strong with determination on a buckskin horse next to Judy on Freckles the strawberry roan. Max is on Daisy the palomino, leading flaxen Danny Boy packed with extra water. The loyal draft horse is eager to fight. He wants to break ahead and stomp all over the enemy. Kristin is trotting past on black Violet.

Wiseoda's warriors ride with all the other tribes in Beautyland and numbering in the thousands. They catch up to Wiseoda for a meeting with Rangers and guard all sides. It is a splendorous sight to see. The Rangers all wear Patriot militia hats and suede-fringed coats over thick durable pants. They have on boots and spurs and are all ready to melt Blaze's army out of existence. The leaders rest in a powwow for a few minutes and then advance through the forest. They cut across snow-covered meadows and partially frozen streams to flat-forested land high above the valley. Treacherous war grounds lie ahead but they move forward in defiance.

Imagining the destruction of such pristine lands exasperates Scout. Evil's devastating plan brought to fulfillment could put an end to everything! His grief turns to anger while thinking about it in flight over the beautiful terrain and he says to himself, "This Beautyland, not be forgotten. I let nothing make it rotten. I meet Chief with Goodman's team for relief. Beautyland, our land, God does understand!"

He zips into a downdraft past a herd of buffalo coming from the plains and warns them, saying, "Steer clear! Go back! Run far away, no good this way! Trust me, Beautyland under attack, must not come, firestorms rain from sea. Go to Beaver Country!"

The buffalo trust him. The alpha bull blows a snorted thank-you as "Yammmoooohhhhh."

The herd rumbles ground in hustling out of there. Scout flies farther and glides above the head of a bear. It skedaddles following the buffalo. He swoops down to the patriots and stops on a branch six feet in the air above the ears of Wiseoda's horse. The eagle-feather headdress worn by the chief intimidates Scout a little. He gives a nervous gulp and says, "I speak with angels. The stallions tell me to stay alert. I tell you, air no longer work, smell deadly at river. Demons come to burn your liver!"

Jake replies, "We know, eagle! We know! Charlie Cavanaugh is taking care of that. Everyone will soon be safe. The Captain will put the island smokestacks out. I hope he finishes before acid rain and brimstone come, but he is on his way. We must quickly beat the invaders here. This is war. Tell the angelic stallions, "We have risen from the shelter." We cannot sit by and wait. We have to help to win this fight. There is no time to waste. The Indians have prepared helmets with gas masks enough for us all. Soldiers in the shelter gave us weapons. We are all ready. We have a plan.

"Tell the great steeds. They will not have to do it alone. We have air, food, and ammunition. These facemasks around our necks and the ones around our horses will provide good air. These walnut wood helmets strung over our backs will protect us from their clubbing lances. The Indians wove reeds for the hoses to our mouthpieces. We have refillable buffalo-skin air-tanks. See the tank tied to my saddle strings. Even our horses will have air. We can fight to the end.

"The underground portals will serve as filling stations to siphon fresh oxygen. The soldiers made pressurized steel drums with pumps at each entrance. The military prepared weapons underground for all able-bodied Beaulancians and the stations are guarded. If the demons invade, our army will melt them away."

Scout asks, "How long will the tank last strong? Will it last to power on long?"

Jake says, "Twelve hours with each fill. We are ready eagle. You stay on that branch and wait! We are going to rig together an outfit for you, victory or death!"

He trots the rugged ranch horse over to a group of squaws and asks them to make a rig to fit Scout. They gather supplies, sit on the ground constructing and soon finish. Jake takes it to Scout, saying, "Beaulancians are one, and every bloodline is linked. We are all for all. Wear the gear and keep scouting. It fits well eagle. Let it hang around your neck until needed! Your small tank will only last four hours. Be on the lookout for filling stations. Here is a little map. Find the stallions and tell them everything!"

Scout nods and flaps away into clean clouds with the tank bulging on his back. He wears the mask and a hose under his chin and a tiny wooden helmet on his head. He circles the sky to watch them leave before zooming away. He wants to inform the celestial steeds up north but flies south instead past the coast to get a look at the navy. The air is thick with fallout. He installs the protective gear to breathe.

Cavanaugh is making good progress on way to the Island. The estimated time of arrival may be tomorrow or the day after. Time quickly passes. Scout refills at a hidden portal near the palisades. He feels a presence and takes to the air. The raven swoops under him to an acacia branch on the edge of a cliff. Scout dives down to rest beside the raven and talks through the mask.

"Raven, why not underground? You live not long. Air breathed in is thickly brown, not clearly thin. Follow me! I show shelter to live through smelter. Without mask for the task raven should stay nicely down safely within."

The raven says, "I am fine! Dittereep, I too can rhyme! Where underground is where you say? I may find a mask to fly away. Dittereep, tell in ground where raven stay. The sea, not calm or green, dark clouds drop yellow flakes, fast and mean. Brimstone falls at will. Beautyland it surely kill, dittereep!"

Scout notices strange red highlights in the center of its eyes, moving like hands. He suspiciously looks closer through the mask, asking, "Do you know Utopio?"

The raven answers, "Utopio who? What do-he-do? Dittereep. Will he fit my head with what you wear so I not dead and cause a tear."

Scout suspects, devious play. By this time, all Beaulancians, especially birds, have heard of Utopio. He distracts the raven by pointing a wing tip at the ground behind him saying,

"What do you know, look before took. A freshly dead rabbit, wouldn't you like to grab it?"

The raven turns to look and Scout skedaddles like a rocket through the night's thick brown clouds. He escapes the chilling raven thinking about devilish fingers waving inside eyes trying to hypnotize. The ill-mannered raven finally turns back around seeing Scout gone and smiles wickedly about it.

The militia and Indians slowly ride through the forest closer to The Spring of Plenty. Jake sees something moving atop a rocky hill. He views it through a spyglass and shouts, "Saber Toes, come here, old pal!"

Scout returns zooming across the sky near the lion. Saber Toes jumps down from one rocky point to another and rests on a boulder near Jake. He speaks sneakily catlike but unafraid, saying,

"Uh, roar dudes and lady people, an army of Lava Clan cover the riverside. Like from the spring, seventy dogs leave and sniff around up here! They have multiple wagons of yellow uneatable cakes parked in a ravine, amigos. The air is bad at the spring, dudes. It burns my throat. Yeah, and a big caped villain dude is in charge. He looks nasty, my folksy-folk dudes. I think we should worry. I would like to stay and watch amigos but this cranky kahuna dude makes even the Lava Clan scared. He has many with him too, duty dudes. I think he's trying to ruin things around here, peoples!"

Scout waits on a branch, letting Saber Toes have the attention. Takoda rides over and says,

"Saber do good! We camp for night."

Jake and Wiseoda agree and appoint sentries. Everyone else dismounts, inspects weapons, and relaxes.

Takoda says, "Time coming soon, Saber, get mean and ready! Squaws make mask. You wear in fight."

The lion understands and does as told. He moves catlike over to the crafty women and paws a hard thick leather mouthpiece. He puts it on and catches a paw nail on the air hose.

He says, "Like, oops, man! I almost killed the snake," meaning the hose.

Behind transparent lenses and muffled under the mask, he says, "All is well, man. It did not tear. Like, this is a tough hose, dudettes!"

He can easily fasten it by sliding the latch in for locking or out to release. He flips his head back dropping the facemask and hose off to a shoulder and with another flip, the whole apparatus is back on. Takoda makes him keep it on. Saber Toes leaps onto the rocks in full battle dress and climbs the hill overlooking the forest.

Scout leaves to scour elsewhere and finds Lucer's search party about fifteen miles away thinking, "*Hmmm, fierce fighting dogs in hills, Blaze in ravine with gorisilles. I check out Blaze before telling all what seen.*"

He hides inside a small thicket without ruffling accumulated yellow flakes listening. Blaze paces back and forth speaking to Red saying,

"No point in staying here. The river is dry."

Red replies, "But the mustangs are all dead. How can we move the wagons?"

Blaze answers, "Get their carcasses unhitched and strap in your gorisilles, you idiot!"

Red asks, "Yes, heinous, of course. Where are we taking the wagons, your majesty?"

Blaze answers, "To the raid on Plentyville and you are now a Lieutenant! Do not dump any here. This is all the supply we have. The dry spring serves no purpose anymore. We will drop some cargo in wells on our way. Any homesteaders alive are probably begging to die. There is no way they can breathe this air. Ha! Ha! Ha! Now go hitch your gorisilles to wagons. We will leave tonight!"

Red asks, "One more thing, your heinous, is everyone to come or should some stay here?"

Blaze says, "Stay here, why? What would they do? You are now a Captain."

Red answers, "Maybe, they would guard the cave?"

Blaze asks, "What is there to guard? The spring is dead and useless. The bad air will soon kill them all anyway. No one but us is going to live. Falling brimstone will be our guard. No one can threaten us. Go prepare for travel!"

Red responds, "Yes you're heinous!"

He organizes a couple of hundred demons, telling them clearly, "I am your newly promoted Captain in charge. You had better obey. Kick the dead horse carcasses aside and hitch yourselves to the wagons."

They follow orders and pass the message down to prepare to move out. Scout overhears and registers the plan in his mind before flapping quietly away. He slows down to look back once more and sort them out. Chief Wiseoda sees him reaching the forest and sticks out an arm. Scout lands on it and shares the whereabouts of Lucer's horde. He tells all he knows about Blaze and the info gives them time to prepare.

Jakes insists, "Let the Lava Clan come. We are more than ready. Scout, I want you to ask Utopio to follow Blaze. When we finish off the dogs we'll head to hill country farms."

He knows how to fight more confidently after winning the battle of the Salt Dome Caverns. Chief Wiseoda flicks his arm and Scout flaps away. It is a long flight to Beaver Dam to look for the celestial horses. He tests the mouthpiece before leaving. Yellow fog grows fast over great portions in route. He worries knowing the southern air is putrid and hopes the northern air is good. He flips on the mask again breathing carefully not to use up the tank too soon.

The Indians and Rangers take positions to ambush the seventy or so, coming gargies. One thousand Indians climb aspens and nestle their water guns on branches. Jake, Will, Hank, Molly, and Ben take cover behind boulders. Judy, Max, and Kristin wait far away downhill with the remaining thousands of Indians. Will hides next to Jake behind a Sequoia near a bluff and says,

"It will be a massacre!"

Jake quietly nods, "yes."

The gargies smell human scents from less than a mile away. Lucer snarls at the pack and says,

"Err-err, ruff, people not far from here."

They spread out sniffing and running over big rocks and around tall trees into the trap. Lucer dodges a water blast shouting,

"Arf-arf, look out! Get away from the trees!"

The gargies run confused with nowhere to escape the forest. Indians fire repeatedly with easy pickings and the battle becomes a slaughter except for Lucer and four other gargies dodging shots.

Hank jumps out from behind a boulder and blasts two down. Ben steps out from behind a Sequoia and blasts two more. Finally, Lucer is the only gargie left alive. He runs down a hill to face thousands of waiting Indians and circles his stance looking for an out. He heads toward a herd of buffalo slowly moving toward higher land.

Max grabs Daisy from a tie line between two trees and chases him for a quarter mile. Lucer leaps off the edge of a narrow canyon trying to make it across. In midair, he looks back and wickedly smirks. Daisy braces for an immediate stop. Max lets him have it in the face with a power blast as he falls. Daisy slides to the edge on her rump. Max dismounts, backs her up and rubs her neck, saying, "A bit more skid and we'd be goners, Daisy girl. Nice save, gal!"

Relief sets in and he hollers, "I got him!"

Lucer fell only twenty feet slamming on a rocky overhanging crag. Max sees his oozing body and leaves meeting Kristin and his Dad hurrying over.

Jake remarks, "You got the last one! Easy does it, right, son? Good job, *oh, man*, I am very proud of you."

Indians extinguish remains of crackling gargie bodies before fires erupt.

Saber Toes watches from the hill without a mask. The air is still good. He comes down to meet the victors as Takoda motions him.

Saber explains, "Kimoheffea'," their leader dude is on the way to Plentyville. Like now is a good time to go after him!"

Wiseoda raises a hand signaling all the tribes and Jake's team to fall in. The full moon darkens from smog as yellow flakes drizzle to the ground. Everyone installs masks before leaving the forest to find Blaze.

Meanwhile, Scout flies through the fallout over vast territories afraid another air tank will empty before making it to Beaver Lake. He already refilled once and the nearest known portal is out of the way to the southwest. His supply has only half an hour remaining when suddenly over Goodman's farm; he notices an air stream pushing smog away from the ground. He flies down to get a better look wondering, *"What is this,"* and finds the secret hatch by the barn ajar.

He acknowledges, "Aha, fresh air! Oh no, did a dare do a sentry here! What happened? Wake up! Wake up! Squawk, squawk!"

Scout sees fang marks on the back of the sentry's neck and prints of three dogs on the ground.

He remarks, "Oh no, trooper dead at the flue. Scout have no weapon and know not what to do. I fill here, hurry there, and hold breath against death. I tweak my beak to hold the hose. Air does bank into the tank. I make fast this filling last and with talon wrenched on portal lid, I close to keep it hid. I go tell steeds of dirty deeds."

Before leaving, he hears a skirmish in the tunnel.

Splish splash arf growl arf splash growl arf ruff uff uffger uff splash. Someone exclaims, "I got the last one!"

The three murderous gargies all die in the wet and wild fight with Beaulancian sentries in the tunnel. Scout flaps up and away through very dense smog and falling flakes. His little wooden helmet covers both ears as winds swish around volcanic ash. He notices Astro walking uncharacteristically remorseful through the now dry riverbed. He visited Colima underground through a portal up river from the spring. After the delightful reunion, he moseys' on down to peek at the spring and finds the dead horse ravine. Their bodies are still warm. He gives last respects and looks up to Folkhaven hoping to see their resurrection but it is too late.

Instead, he sees Scout flapping across the brown sky wearing strange headgear. He lifts off in super mode to catch him. He swoops his long neck under Scout and with a few swirls of mane wraps him on securely. A cool tingly rescued feeling rustles feathers on his head. He speaks through the mouthpiece sounding to Astro as, "Hallelujah, stud, I needed a ride," but in reality he said, "Hey ya bud, my feet ya tied!"

Astro lunges powerfully to the stars above the storm into solar light. Scout is ecstatic and removes his mask to talk asking, "Eee, he, ha, ha, fresh air, do I dare? Ah, it is good air up here. Fun to the moon we dun! I cannot believe nor did I perceive where Astro are we steed?"

He answers, "Safe in the high light. Where were you going with that helmet tonight? Tell me Scout, what is it you know all about? I cannot rest until you shout. Eeegalala, whinninnineee, I am sad myself but never fear the end is near. Blaze Evil will soon disappear."

Scout explains all and Astro says, "Be not afraid! Spirit is in control of the Dam.

Beaver Lake is free from worry. Utopio is preparing the master plan. You need not care to scurry. Ride me safely wearing what you can."

They drift down from the galaxy toward Spirit standing atop Beaver Bridge. He watches reddish brimstone raining far away over the dark ocean. Astro soars back through the atmosphere. Spirit sees a little alien riding his neck. It is belly down gripping his blue mane.

Astro asks, "Hello, Spirit, could you undo Scout, please?"

Spirit asks, "Scout, is that Scout? Let me see!"

He pulls off Scout's no-longer-needed mask and helmet with his teeth. Scout says, "See, it is me. Untangle the mane please. Gee whiz. I went higher than an eagle's biz."

Spirit remarks, "The outer limits have served you well. Even your speech is better now."

He helps him down to a rail on the bridge. Scout wobbles taking deep breaths while explaining past events to Spirit.

Spirit explains, "Utopio has been diligently digging in the land of limestone, enlarging quarries, to fill a clear supersize craft made from only breath. His legend continues. I tell you, he is the most gifted stallion you will ever know. He achieved creating the largest wagon ever imagined.

He did?" asks Scout?

Spirit says, "It holds enough lime to cover a trillion acres and has no apparent frame. It is too large to detect in the sky and carries what looks like brown clouds. It slips undetectable under smog and blocks fallout. He harnessed himself to pull it. Wherever seen, the storm is not the storm, but he. Blaze only thinks it is his wicked storm. Utopio made Beautyland safe and Blaze has no idea!"

Scout asks, "How happens this contraption?"

Spirit describes, "Well, first, Utopio spun himself centrically like a tornado. He caused enough friction to turn crushed stone glowing hot and made good quicklime. He pulls strings with his teeth to open turbines and powerfully squirts caulking into wells. Well moisture when it meets quicklime causes solidified protective coverings over each well. He is an excellent shot with tubes extending the reach. Utopio prevents soil and ground water contamination. The cart neutralizes Sulfur Dioxide as it pushes it back across the sea to the island."

Scout states, "The storm can do no harm, thanks to Utopio who has not even an arm!"

Spirit replies, "The dirty brownish yellow fallout seen sprinkling everywhere is only lime dust. It is important to keep it out of your eyes, nose, mouth and skin but it will actually bring new life to the soil. Blaze is going to hate that. At this very moment, Utopio's cart is more than half over the ocean and only partly remaining over Beautyland filtering the storm. Have no fear Beauty is safe."

Astro adds, "I wonder about the cleanup. How will it all go away?"

Spirit states, "The lime drops through perforations but the cart vacuums it up again. Utopio shifts it back and forth over the area. It looks like fallout when actually rising. No one can tell the difference. On and off the ground again eludes everyone. The cart has multiple blades churning smog through the lime filtering out toxins. Roller presses and cutters reduce the lime into little flaky pieces. Great big fans blow clean and pressed flakes through the perforations.

"It appears dangerous but not in reality. The craft distributes lime as a big sifter in the sky. Keep your helmet on until Utopio is completely over the ocean and you will be all right. Rinse affected areas thoroughly with water if a burning sensation occurs. Between what is real and perceived only we know the difference, Scout. It has to be this way for a while yet."

Chapter 21

BATTLE FOR FARMS

The militia feels stronger winds and cooler fallout gathering around. Takoda dismounts after a long bareback riding night and sits on soft ashy ground under a tree. There in the same tree is Saber Toes, cat-napping on a branch. Vision is poor in the ashy lime blizzard, but Saber awakes with Takoda's scent near and says through his mask, "Well hey, Takoda, *quepaso*? We are near the farmlands on down the easy rolling hills, dude. The destroyer is marching onward with treacherous troops, dude!"

Takoda responds, "Umph, I need know how far from farms. Is time we leave forest? Ug, need more oxygen. Find air, Saber, I tell tribes refill now. We refill, circle Blaze, and ambush. We get ready. You watch, tell more, when know more!"

Astro leaves Scout at the dam with Spirit and flies high in a gallop over Utopio's cart. Using angelic inside light his eyes penetrate through the lime machine. He sees Jake on the forest floor with the militia and zooms under the cart, shouting, "Ehhennie, whinnie, whin, whin!" He flies through the fallout and lands in front of the Rangers' saying, "Goody Goodman, Jake and company, listen! I have news. Gather around to hear my plan."

Astro needs to be clear and performs only slightly saying,

"The air is soon to be good again, 'oh-happy-day, oh-happy-day', right? Utopio is blocking the volcanic storm. Do not ask how, no time to waste, I come only to inform."

The Beaulancians rest and listen to unmasked Astro speak. He penetrates their souls with an angelic voice encouraging trust and hope saying, "The Presidents army is not capable to see in this poor visibility. They hear very well and I will give them know how. You must refill and surround the farms! Blaze's evil forces cannot see their own noses on their own faces. The darkness of night will last all day."

Utopio's craft fills the sky and only occasional rays of sunlight let in between lime drifts. They all ride to portals. Takoda brings the Rangers to a portal near his old campground and Wiseoda leads thousands in another direction. Thanks to Utopio's foresight, there is enough for all.

Jake asks Astro, "My friend, may I mount you? I would like a look at the battlefield from above?"

He replies, "Ehennennie, whinnie, whin, mount on, General and I will show it!"

He does on the first try with his hands on the stud's back and a jump from a boulder. His arms float freely at his sides. Astro slowly lifts off the ground, gliding only high enough not to bump heads into Utopio's cart.

"Are you all right, General," he asks

Jake says, "I am fine! Can you take us any faster?"

Astro asks, "How tight can you hold on? Take my mane in both hands and squeeze your legs on my sides. I will show you the end of hazy weather."

His mane grows bundling into a saddle under Jake. Cool blue tail strands travel under the stud's girth making a belt over his lap. Jake receives the VIP treatment complete with stirrups and a horn to hold onto. Jake has a rope and drops it over the horn. Astro asks one more time if he is ready before really stepping up to speed. He adjusts his seat and says, "Yes, a bit nervous though. Whenever you say go, I am ready!"

Astro replies, "Go," and darts away with an arched back under the bottom of the sky wagon. His hooves run along its rounded bottom and push off higher to blue skies.

Astro sings, "Beautyland, O Beautyland, start spreadin' the views, it's up to you, Beautyland. These, bag a blond blues, are longing for hay. It is up to you, Plentyville watcher. It's up to you little Plentyville watcher you."

Jake instructs, "Astro, circle over those bean fields."

He glides quietly above heads of marching beasts. Jake looks down and sees Blaze for the first time ahead of a couple of thousands beasts and says, "Take me ahead to see the terrain they follow."

The super stud says, "In a no lackaday split I will!"

Astro amazes himself simulating a horse size firefly. He gracefully arcs in flight with a glowing tail and Jake sees the landscape is all farms.

He explains, "Here is what I think, Astro. We will fight before Blaze dumps those wagons somewhere. We cannot afford to let him reach the higher plateau and get lost or ruin the Plenty Valley. Unfortunately, houses, trees and crops cover this lower land too. But the hills surrounding it work well for a fast and thorough ambush."

Astro adds, "Elevation drops in the war zone to the southeast."

Jake replies, "The vast plateau gradually slopes south to the Plenty Valley. We could possibly catch runaways on the plateau before they reach the steep drop off at rim country. Precious corn and cotton fields and orchards of various kinds grow in the Plenty Valley. We want to save them from destruction if possible. Then just after is Plentyville. Nope, I am sure of it. The hill country farmlands are best for battle. There we have a chance to keep them from escalating it into something worse."

Up to high altitude again under the cart provides a greater view of all of Beautyland. Astro uses special eyes as flash through the fallout for Jake to see. The Evils at low altitude think the flashes are glimpses of volcanic eruptions. Utopio pulls the smog purifier farther out to sea against the volcanic smog. The air becomes lighter as fallout over the battleground slightly clears. Backdrafts will keep it coming for a while longer.

Jake insists, "Take me back, Astro. I have seen enough."

He reroutes in majestic flight carrying him to a point in the atmosphere above Utopio. His cousin Utopio glows an unhealthy pure yellow among the dry falling flakes while pushing the cart. Astro flies up to good clean air above the storm and rests.

Jake takes his mask off and breathes in the fresh air, saying,

"Riding you is nothing like any horse I have ever ridden. Nothing in the world is more fun than galloping through thin air. We need your help now more than ever. The blessings of Beauty must remain intact. Bring me down!"

Astro responds, "Wait General, not yet, a closer look, you get."

He rides beneath the floating cart and looks at Evil's horse. Black Rain is fierce.

Jake asks, "Can they see us?

Astro answers, "No what they see is only an aurora of light dancing through the thick air and have no idea what to make of it.

Jake responds, "Astro, we must return!"

He stubbornly zooms over Utopio's cart again to demonstrate the stars from a global perspective. "These stars have a purpose. Everything God made is good, Mr. Goodman."

"Even Blaze?" asks Jake?"

Astro says," He is a creation with free will. He chose to use it against the creator since being against what is good. This is what Blaze is about so stay on guard. He may know your name. He has fun turning what is good into bad."

Jake remarks, "The cart looks small from here. I see streamers of smog spewing from the island ahead of Utopio. I can barely see his body. He looks like a spot of fire. This height really makes me dizzy."

Astro adds, "Utopio looks harnessed to the whole sky. Can you see the navy getting closer to the Island? Now, hold on to your hat."

They return to the ground, helmet and all. Jake dismounts and Takoda says through his mask, "Jake, come, I take you to refill tank and you tell me what you saw."

Twenty minutes later, they return.

Jake says to all, "I have much to tell. Sit on the ground and gather for a powwow. This is what I know. Our enemies' eyes let them down. They cannot see well through the smog. At least one hundred poisonous wagonloads move slowly west. Large furry beasts two thousand strong with hordes of dangerous dogs are marching to hill country farms. The caped devil leads on a fiercely determined black stallion. It appears meaner than I have ever seen a horse. I have good news though. The air will soon be clean.

"Utopio is stopping the fallout. In an hour or less, we will no longer need our tanks. Nevertheless, wear the masks to protect your face from flying acidic dust. We will see clearly enough in battle as the weather changes."

Wiseoda asks, "How great general you want Shashouix tribe to attack."

Jakes instructs, "Wiseoda, you will bring the Shashouix around the battlefield with me to the west. We will split up in the western hills before the enemy gets there. Your warriors will attack from the south-eastern hills. My division will attack from the west. I will need at least four hundred of your warriors. The other tribes will divide here. Some will charge from this northern side while the others attack from the northeastern rear. A company under the command of newly appointed Colonel Will Marsh will remain here in reserve. Will, congratulations, you protect the woman and children. Position scouts to watch the battle and be on guard!"

"Yes, sir, we can talk about retirement benefits later. Thank you, sir," Will replies.

Jake explains, "Warriors are to strike on signal from Takoda's flaming arrow beginning with the northeastern rear. Destroy the drivers and take the wagons. The rest of us will fight in waves sending one group at a time to save reserves. Chiefs, go now and prepare your divisions."

Ten thousand resound, "Yes!"

Their masked exuberant voices roar in rally throughout the forest. Kristin looks around fearfully through her goggles and says with a finger over her mouthpiece, "Shish, not so loud!"

Wiseoda assigns braves around Jake's family. He instructs them to obey Will Marsh. Jake switches horses. He takes the packs off Danny Boy and saddles him for war against Black Rain.

Judy says, "Darling, I love you. I pray we will all be seeing each other again very soon. Keep your weapons full."

"I love you too, honey. Max, hold on to Lady and keep her here," insists Jake.

He kisses Judy and Kristin goodbye and says to Max, "You are the man now son. Stand up straight and look after our family."

He shakes his hand like a man but hugs him goodbye like a son. He mounts stout Danny Boy who since a colt has waited to be a hero. Jake trained him for battle at a young age. This is his big chance to see some real action. The Goodman family and Molly leave with Will to safety in the deeper forest. Kristin reunites with Charlie Cavanaugh's motherless son Thomas at a camping spot. They like each other very much but Max steals attention away.

The chiefs return from organizing and bargaining with tribes- men. They declare loyalty as a united nation under Wiseoda and Jake. They understand the mission in full readiness.

Jake speaks loudly saying, "Beaulancians, a dangerous folk we are! Fear not the enemy, Almighty God is on our side! Do you have the will to win?"

Wiseoda shouts, "We will not lose!"

Jake hollers, "Evil is doomed. Conquer them to hell! Your weapons are mighty against them. We shall overcome. Angels are on our side. This beautiful land is ours to keep. Protect Beauty! This is our dimension and God's grace forever shines on it. Do not be afraid, fight with might. We are a powerful force, ee-ha!"

He spurs Danny Boy to the lead. A contagious thunderous romp ensues as so many leave to circle the enemy. The demons howl gargled yodels giving praise to blaze the conqueror while they march. They drown out the heavy hooves encircling them.

Soon the big charge will come. The poorly organized gorisilles are bad scouts. Gargies are usually better. Their sense of smell deteriorated in the fallout. An attack is rising yet they have no idea. Nevertheless, they are somewhat stupid anyway. Up and down hills through tall trees and red rocks around the battle zone, mounted warriors jump creeks and ditches to find positions. They ride through dusty fallout, over downed branches and lime-covered rocks. The flaky fallout blocks their travel from sight. An Evil scouting party of gargies led by Red is beyond the front in rendezvous to the plateau.

Jake is aware and tells Hank, "Take a party of braves and track them down."

Hank asks, "How many dogs?"

He answers, "By the looks of these tracks, I would guess at least twenty. Get going, Hank, you have the advantage."

Hank selects twenty Shashouix braves, without a doubt the best warriors in Beautyland. He carefully steers them uphill west into juniper country. He spots Red through a spyglass, sitting on the ground under a tree eating something. It is a large spoiled bird egg, steamed cooked by his breath. He holds twenty dogs on chain leashes sitting on duffs eating other dead birds and spoiled eggs. These birds died before Scouts rescuers could save them from the poisoned River.

Hank signals his team to encircle the area. One brave, faces a challenging pit bull. He fires a wet arrow into its mouth. The gargie dies, but others rush forth angrily dripping from frothy fangs. One metal tooth dog leaps at the bowman and sets his saddle on fire with glowing hot teeth. Another brave douses it from behind. Hank's shooter leaks under his arm just in time to catch a dog going beneath his horse.

"Got ya," he says and rides fast over to another entanglement with braves. He pumps the water shooter trigger wildly in all directions and wets the gargies lurking in fog. Splashes and growling and simmering sounds of hit beasts fill the air as *Splish, splash, arf, arf, ziss-zysszle,-sizzs!*

In seconds, all the hounds are dead. Red is nowhere though. He escaped. The band rides in and out of junipers, searching. Then suddenly, Hank sees bright red fur coiled under the low branches of a tree. He points his water gun saying, "Come out of there or die where you are."

Red crawls out groveling in a harsh voice, "Wait! Don't shoot, I can be friendly."

Hank says to five nearby Indians, "He is bigger than one brave can handle. Team up and move him over here. Now tell me, gorisille, what do they call ya?"

"Hiccup, I am called Red," he answers.

Hank says, "No foolin'! I bet that's because of your fine red hair now, ain't it?"

Red exclaims with a whimper, "No, you're heinous, because of my nose. I drink too much."

He says no more but jumps without another word above the saddle fenders to punch Hank's head off. Hank leans out of the way and squirts him down. Red falls dying with his last words,

"Um-ooie, I liked duck," and his lights go out.

Meanwhile, Jake, Wiseoda, Takoda, Ben, and a band of three thousand make headway across the front.

Jake peers through a spyglass finding warrior divisions around the battlefield saying, "The storm has lessened but the demons' have poor eyesight anyway."

Blaze is prancing on Black Rain through a field heading to a distant house. Wiseoda raises his hand to a warrior, saying,

"Take eight hundred braves to the east side."

Jake says to Wiseoda, "This is where I stay to fight the front. Leave me warriors. Ben, you cut out four hundred more and keep the plateau safe from escaping monsters."

"Yes, sir, General," he says.

He waves his hand to direct a section out and they willingly group behind him.

Jake looks through the spyglass, saying,

"Takoda, when Blaze is only three hundred yards from this hill fire the signal arrow and charge. We will wait until after your advance for Blaze to get closer. Warriors wet your arrows and ready yourselves. Keep them busy."

Wiseoda answers, "The great spirit will guide us to victory."

Jake acknowledges saying, "Don't forget, let the warriors at rear charge the buckboards before getting too anxious. Advance one hundred yards later. Measure their strength a little at a time. Keep divisions in reserve and send new barrages every thirty minutes.

"Replaced waves can take care of wounded while relay waves fight until called on again. Rotate the waves repeatedly if the battle lasts long and let us hope not. Our progress will dictate future strategy. They may be more dangerous than we think. If so, run to the nearest portals. Protect the irrigation ditches from hazardous chemicals. We need fresh water to kill these monsters.

"I will be after Blaze. The first one to kill him gets five acres of my land. If he does get away, follow my tracks. My eyes will stick to him. I will not wait for anyone. If you lose me, ride through Harmos Ravine, I will most likely be there. It is a shortcut to Plenty Ville. Stay on guard, Blaze may use it too, questions anyone?"

No one asks or argues. They extend palms to shake farewell and divide. Meanwhile, Hank's small party rides on the plateau toward the ridge over the ravine to keep watch. The enemy steadily approaches the firing line. The countdown to battle begins. Blaze is three hundred yards away from Jake. Takoda fires the signal arrow and as expected, the northeastern warriors attack their buckboards. The gorisilles stop pulling. Indians rush in from all sides drawing chaotic attention. The enemy is in disarray with surprise.

Blaze cries, "I am seeing things. This is not happening."

Heavy horses pound soft farm dirt and dusty lime rises all around. The Indian's masks suppress their hollers. The rear assault plunges spears and arrows at harnessed gorisilles and fierce gargies jump at horse throats. On higher ground, Wiseoda watches the first wave dodge and dilute sulfur balls with squirts and explains, "Enemy strong, swing lasers like tomahawks."

A Shashouix brave douses an arrow under the nozzle of his water skin and shoots a demon attacking another warrior on a bean field. Wiseoda raises and lowers his hand signaling reinforcements to attack forty gorisilles ganging up on a small group of warriors.

He shouts, "Save arrows, use squirters!"

They kill them all as even greater numbers dwindle into smelly lava across the battlefield. One large monster slings his arm across the neck of a mounted brave saying, "Issand taur eekand ahtow. This land is my land now," and with one hand, he knocks the Indian's head off. Another fearless dry gun Indian jumps off his horse with a large knife and puts it into the demon's back. The demon spins him around to his wide-open mouth and crushes his head. Takoda saw this and says, "Great spirit, ride with me."

He dodges lasers by sliding to the side of his bareback horse and goes after the beast. He plugs two wet arrows into him for the kill and squirts three others dead. The war battles on with slurping and sizzling sounds as enemies die. Few warriors suffer pain. Too many have died. An angered brave hears a guttural war cry, "Chuh ach dung wo! You must die!"

He charges a pack of gargies ready to attack wounded warriors and pumps repeating streams into them. He switches to wet arrows with both hands free from reins. The wounded are saved and the wave changes. During the second wave, Wiseoda sees Jake's access to Blaze blocked by guards. The general has not had a clear way since the battle started. He killed many gargies and gorisilles yet never able to reach Blaze. He is now closer than ever.

Wiseoda shouts, "Eee-yahh," and kicks into a full gallop to help.

More than a hundred gorisilles and over fifty fang-ready gargies guard Blaze. Jake kills several with the help of two-dozen warriors. He finds additional courage seeing Wiseoda killing many on his way in. Jake kills two with one shot but the guards still outnumber them. Wiseoda calls out to other nearby warriors, "Help us, we get Blaze."

Danny Boy finally sees Black Rain through a space in the fighting crowd. He really wants a piece of him and escapes dozens of attacking beasts as Jake shoots them dead from the saddle. Now the Indians have cut down most of the guards near Blaze. Danny Boy rears to full height pointing his hooves at Black Rain's chest. Blaze shoots flames from five-finger tips and torches him.

Jake jumps to the ground spraying his hide. Black Rain casts a red laser spell into Danny Boy's eyes causing him to run into a rock solid wall at a vacant farmhouse. He breaks his neck, and dies. Blaze turns to Jake to cause something similar but the mask protects his eyes. Jake fires a water blast and the cape blocks it. Blaze kicks Black Rain into a run to dry the cape in warm sunnier wind. The air is changing to almost normal. The cape water evaporates. He reaches far out of sight over a small rolling hill and Jake shouts, "You won't get away!"

A close brave lifts Jake by an arm to the back of his horse. They fend off lasers, dust balls, and clubs with anxious squirts killing all in the way. The soft-mouthed Indian ponies twist and turn in battle without need of reins to steer. The braves tap heels on their sides to indicate direction and shoot accurate shots with both hands. They kill many more demons. Fankdustles are the enemy's all-in-one dust ball thrower, sword like lance, and staff used for walking or bludgeoning. They fire laser rods and electric rays out the tips. It is the latest device invented by Cain for this invasion. He had great pleasure testing them on gargies. The clearing sky improves enemy's vision. They beat on warriors' legs, stomachs, and heads in close combat and fire lasers more accurately. The Indians suffer greater casualties. Water weapons are going dry.

They fight off huge beasts with spears and dry arrows. Gargies are going under horses and biting their legs. Gorisilles are out maneuvering them and the battlefield is a riot of anger. Crowds of attackers on both sides fight ruthlessly. Downed braves hop up behind other riders in greater numbers. Some stand on bare backs to reach tall gorisilles while others slide to horse sides avoiding attacks. Fankdustles fire many crisscrossing lasers in the air. Takoda ducks and shoots a stream in the barrel of a fankdustle saying, "Let your red light burn through," and because wet it does.

He runs to an irrigation ditch filling his shooter alongside many other braves. He takes out four more beasts and races over to help Jake fend off other dangerous gorisilles. Fankdustles come swinging at them and fire rays in every direction. Jake blasts into thinner air reflecting blue, green, yellow and red spectrums in the new sunshine and several die. Yapping gargies attack riders with all fours off the ground. Maimed warriors suffer mangled and burnt tissues. The beasts cause blistering exchanges in the second wave; nevertheless, the tribesmen eliminate most and put the flaming crops out too.

Some tribes wear painted guardian symbols on their bodies. The significance of these designs foils gorisilles. Beasts stand still at the sight better than hypnosis. Slight glances cause wacky shots at each other. The warriors believe in what the symbols represent not in how they appear. The air reeks of rotten eggs as dead drivers and poisonous burning wagons ignite. Masks cannot conceal the smell. The second wave gathers wounded warriors as beast's retreat. The determined warriors have outfought the brutish demons.

Jake hollers to Wiseoda through the noise, "I am over here. Save your resources. I am going after Blaze. I will get him."

Blaze heard and shouts from above the southern battlefield, "I will burn you down!"

He turns himself into a wide and long serpent mustering up a fire from within and blows it out his mouth setting the bean field ablaze. Jake chases in the direction on a new mount followed by a small band on fast-frightened horses. They only saw flames shooting down from higher land but not Evil as himself emitting the torch from his mouth while hidden on the ground on his belly in true snake like form.

The third wave wades into deadly smoke from burning buckboards and works on putting fires out. A mixture of water shooter sprays and backdrafts from Utopio's cart smothers fires. Indians overturn hazardous waste, salvage buckboards, and hitch up horses. They drive wounded to underground sanctuaries and take the dead to high forest burial sites. Wiseoda reunites with his warriors and heads to the ravine. Will watches with woman and children on the northwestern rim. When the battlefield settles they head with protective warriors to the far side of Plentyville.

Another tribal chief speaks from atop a high mound on the north side of the battleground saying, "We no see more fighting beasts and Evil leader gone. I go with band southeast and guard platinum ship at coast. No need for masks, air is good!"

The surviving monsters have dispersed somewhere above the hills onto the plateau. Takoda speaks to a warrior saying, "Jake not seen anywhere. Hank and Ben gone to Rim Country, we follow father through ravine. "

Demonic tracks leading into the ravine disappear on a curve toward Plentyville. The army exits portals into fresh air near the city. Charlie Cavanaugh is out to sea. Utopio pushes smog slowly behind the navy. The air over the ocean is thick and dangerous. Charlie's flotilla is running at full steam. He says to another officer on his helm deck, "When we get there, it's as good as over, over there!"

Chapter 22

RESTRAINT

Cavanaugh aboard the good ship *Harmony* signals the flotilla to divide into eight positions around Relief Island. They close in at slow steam to anchor near the shore in blinding Sulfur Dioxide smog. It spreads evenly over the ocean, fills the sky, and smells outrageous. Winds blow red embers of lava streams and brimstone rains from a multitude of volcanic stacks. The fiery lights give the navy some visibility to navigate. Violent volcanic explosions send shivers into morale.

Charlie instructs a Commander Wesson, "Tell the crew we are up against Evil odds, but we are going to win!"

"Aye, aye, sir," he says.

Charlie continues watching the horizon from his balcony.

Meanwhile, the island's Lava Clan sits underground keeping their furry hides away from blazing brimstone battering's and lizards line the shore and rocks across the island. On bare slate floors, females repair dog leather outfits with horsehair-threaded platinum needles. Youngsters wait in romp rooms playing 'Toss the Lava Fire.' Some gorisilles practice whip proficiency and wrestle. Others simply watch the matches eating pumice as if it were popcorn. Enslaved mustangs wait in tight chambers. Human slaves are secluded under a mound near a gully to the rising tide. They eat stolen watermelons from Beautyland and an abundance of kelp.

Commander Wesson worries, not knowing the odds. He understands water's effect on the enemy but knows little about their numbers and nothing about fankdustles. Wesson has no idea what it is like to stand next to a gargie or gorisille. Their smell is horrendous and their sizes are terrifying. Charlie has second thoughts about letting him on the shore with this demonstrated apprehension. Although, Charlie has not experienced the diverse fankdustle weaponry, he does suspect their home turf is more dangerous. However, with winning confidence, he assures Wesson, "No matter what, water is all it takes to put them down."

The commander has no battle experience whatsoever. He knows one side must have the upper hand. Water is easy to fire and it soaks in quickly. Then suddenly a volcanic blast booms and shoots horrendous chunks of brimstone into the ocean.

Charlie picks up a bullhorn and speaks to crews on lower decks, "Fall in line, listen up! I want four boson mates per skiff and nearly a thousand sailors on shore in the next thirty minutes, is that clear? Bring enough ammo to refill each sailor at least once. For God's sake, do not capsize. Bosons listen up. Drop the sailors off and row back fast to pick up another thousand. Today we fight like buccaneers!"

Commander Wesson repeats the orders with a bullhorn, saying to all ships within range, "Duty calls!"

The nearest vessel passes the message on. Soon all the ships' skiffs are loaded and ready to disembark.

Charlie asks, "Ensign Fulbright is my skiff prepared?"

She says, "Aye, aye, sir,"

He goes downstairs to the main deck.

Fulbright enlists elite mates and bosons for Charlie. Crews remaining aboard steamers attach hoses to cisterns and lower primed barrels of sublime lime onto supply boats. Once the first dockers secure landing stations, the depth charges will come. Admiral Charlie orchestrates sending ashore guided hoses.

He shouts, "Now hear this! Bosons' first class, staff your skiffs. Seamen, hold the hoses through the surf and pull ashore!"

They climb down rope ladders into the boats. Charlie seats himself in the especially designated skiff with four Bosons, beautiful Ensign Fulbright and an elite crew of buccaneer fighters. The eight steamers unload ten skiffs, with four bosons, two officers and ten seamen each. They handle five oars per side with one boson mate overseeing the direction and another operating a tiller.

〰

Over tall surges with fierce choppy waves the eighty skiffs row. They bounce and glide furiously while holding hoses in each vessel one-quarter mile to the rocky shore. Admiral Charlie is of the first one hundred sailors to step onto Relief's unholy ground.

He shouts, "We have no shelter here, sailors! Take this land and make it submit. It is all or nothing."

〰

Skiffs stop short of natural rock barricades. Sailors climb overboard into the surf and swim with oxygen helmets on. They cling to slippery sea rocks in crashing waves. Lizards scramble into holes all over the island. The first Dockers hoist ropes to surfing heads and haul struggling sailors ashore. Charlie walks over oyster shells and black sea urchins through poor visibility into barren rocky land. He walks back to the beach, finds a clear spot, and calls a meeting. Officers getting back land legs come from the shore to discuss tactics and strategy.

The Admiral instructs, "Shield your eyes from enemy eyes. Do not look into their eyes. Pass that on to everyone and do not worry about being quiet. They know we are here. Is everyone present and accounted for? There are lizard droppings everywhere. Watch your step. If you brought your pistols then use them on the varmints. "

The long dark-haired ensign beauty answers, "Aye, sir, in only moments all the men will be here sir! More and more skiffs unload every minute, sir!"

The officers disperse. Suddenly, two gorisilles from under a flat rock pop up and both whack Charlie's head with fankdustles. Ensign Fulbright watches. She screams but quickly grabs the handle of her water shooter and blasts them. Charlie's steel helmet barely saves him from those powerful platinum fankdustle bams. The dents look like a deep cross.

"Good job, Ensign. Stick around," he adds.

"Aye, aye, sir, and this water gun really works," she says.

"Indeed," Charlie replies.

They watch seamen tug hoses up volcanic hills from shore shooting pistols similar to colts, one handedly, at dragon lizards and smaller ones crawling over the whole island like rats. The heavy canvas and brass hose holds afloat as a pipeline from ships to skiffs and over land. Nearly two thousand sailors now traverse the island. Hundreds grab hose lengths running up to hatches. The magically dusted lime puts out the attended volcanos, one at a time, and hose handlers cheer, "Smoke's out!"

The extinguishing formula pumps out around the island from multiple ship cisterns and popping lava streams simmer down. Charlie's guardians commandeer parked buckboards. They round up all existing mustangs and attach them to haul depth charges. An eighteen-dog pack, protecting salvage yards, attacks them before getting away. Fulbright collapses as her pants tug between the fangs of a large gargie. It drags her until thirty sailors surround it blasting away. Charlie kills seven dogs coming out a hole. One grabs his facemask with its teeth and pulls it off to the ground.

"Die, you demon mutt," shouts a shooting sailor. Lizards try to run up his legs. He grabs with his uniform gloves on some of the molten gargies remains that he just killed and rubs it on his pants. The lizards jump off with biting-burned tongues and spitting. They run back into holes underground. The sailor's pants are protected well enough with the militaristic durable precautions in place and the magic Utopio dust blessings before battle and will not burn. The horrendously gruesome teeth of the lizards are unable to penetrate the cloth but get a sizzling surprise from the taste. He grabs more molten waste off another dead gargie jackal and runs over to Charlie. He proceeds patting down the Admiral's pants doing the same for him and Charlie's lizard's drop off. Witnesses pass word of the technique in a message chain to every sailor and they simultaneously flee the lizards away all over the island killing demons and lizards readily. After all these years of living with the brutal gargies and gorisilles on the Island of Relief and putting up with their abuse ever since the punishment began the lizards now come to find out their fate is to face death at the monsters mere taste. The evil had gotten into them. The curse said that if any became associates they would be cursed. The lizards have been cursed. The gargies and gorisilles now kill them off by just inflicting a taste to their tongues. They once had fed on dead gargies to stay alive and grow in number but that was before any of the beasts ever died by contact with pure water and molted into hot purple coal-lava.

Charlie speaks to the young buccaneer, "Thank you, what's your name, son?"

The young staff salutes smiling and says, "Master Chief Petty Officer James Duncan, sir!"

"Well, Duncan, you serve me proud, son. I will not forget you young man. Come now and help me get the horses hitched."

"Yes sir! Follow me sir!" Another sailor shows him a fine sorrel and white pinto stallion.

He grabs its mane leaping on and rides it back into battle.

Available crewmembers board rescued slaves onto skiffs and transport them to infirmaries on steamers. Nurses provide medical attention, nourishment, and rest. Tired horses pull the buckboards loaded with depth charges to interior volcano hatches. The drivers blast down beasts in all directions.

Charlie rides up to a sailor holding a hose and asks, "How's your water supply, son?"

The sailor answers, "I'm using my spare skin now, sir!"

The Admiral replies, "OK! Well, put a load on anything that has no whites of eyes, anyway. More water is arriving. You be ready to get to the beach before you run out, sailor."

Charlie opens the five-foot square platinum hatch for the hose handlers to spew down very carefully. They plunge the concoction through and the volcano fizzes. Charlie then rides back down following the hose and another handler says, "Admiral, sir, when they come up from holes in this smog, it is very hard to see them, sir!"

Charlie agrees, "Go on, sailor!"

"Yes sir, thank you, sir. If we miss and shoot a buccaneer, sir, well, sir, remember it is only water, right, sir? I mean you would not prosecute for that, right, sir?"

Charlie responds, "The water blesses us, sailor, and the blood with blessed water saves us. Do not worry, son. To be able to fight with this harmless liquid is a gift. It ends wicked lives yet only washes us cleaner."

"Thank you, sir, watch out, three dogs behind you and more on the side,"

Splishsplashsplashsplashsplashsplashsplash

Between the two of them and a chain of sailors holding the hose, they kill ten gargies and forty gorisilles in the dark. Volcanic stacks firing brimstone reflect on the platinum fankdustles and give them away. Battle sounds boom, swoosh, and sizzle!

Charlie acknowledges, "I got four and you were excellent, son. Keep up the good work."

A half-alive gorisille crawls onto a young hose handler's leg. It reaches an outstretched arm for his neck. Fulbright comes running.

"Zap, splash, there went another one. Be careful, Admiral!"

Four buccaneers behind her shoot another eight gargies and five gorisilles.

She remarks, "They just keep popping up after I'd swear I got them all! They hard to see in this volcanic smoke"

Charlie adds, "Luckily, their stench gives them away even inside these masks."

Gorisilles plunge hard sulfuric bombs down from hills. Charlie and Fulbright climb a rocky abandoned wagon trail to find cover.

Charlie says, "This place gives me the creeps."

When suddenly a female gorisille or gorimille pops up squeezing him and Fulbright squirts her down.

"Admiral, she was close enough to kiss you!"

"She-devils, woo! It tried to eat my face off. That was close!"

"I can only imagine how scary it was, sir!"

"It attacked like a blond sasquatch, with a scarred furry face, human like nose and distinctively female shape. Her eyes were green and twirling like a merry-go-round. Any more time and it could have hypnotized me. Stay on guard, Ensign," he advises.

At this moment, the fight is raging and the brave sailor's progress toward victory even in the darkness. The colorful ammunition reflects in smog. Yellow, red, green, blue and white fankdustle firings glow through water sprays. Enemy victims lay syrupy hot all around. Seamen carefully avoid stepping on patches while dodging a seemingly unending supply of live ones.

Falling brimstone, lights up the smoky brown sky. Charlie dismounts and pulls his horse under a ledge extending from the slope of a volcanic cone. He ropes Fulbright's waist during fast flashes and reels her in under cover for safety. He puts his arm around her offering assurance,

"Ensign, what is your first name?"

She covers her face, "Britty, sir."

Charlie the widower says, "Britty! Hmm, I like that! You are a sight to cause sore eyes in the mask. Luckily, it protects your beautiful eyes. Where are you from, Britty?"

"Grassy Meadows, in Applebee, sir."

Acidic dust balls swish by.

Charlie reacts quickly. "They're getting closer, take cover."

Brimstone bounces and Fulbright's pants catch fire. She squirts them out with her pump gun. Buckboards loaded with depth charges rush up inland slopes as buccaneers fight on defending the cargo. They push barrels inside hatches and explosive lights pop out volcano stacks. Charlie catches glimpses of the topography and finds direction. Water blasters continue diffusing fankdustles. The barrels drain onto gorisille hands killing them instantly.

Commander Wesson orders a team of buccaneers, "Get back to the *Harmony*! Get more hoses and siphon the sea. We will power spray them down by the pack full."

"Yes, sir, right sir, we're on our way, sir!"

Gorisilles blow powder off palms into sailors' faces. Oxygen masks filter the soot before inhaled and protect their eyes.

Charlie shouts, "Spray the dust. It will dilute it into an ointment for sores."

Medics collect the sulfuric paste, adding petroleum jelly, water and iodine, to cover burns. Zooming lasers strike many buccaneers and the injuries are serious. People go down with holes burnt clean through their chests. Occasionally, sailors' uniforms ignite causing painful burns. The demons strike sailors with fankdustle clubs in fierce close combat. Britty returns to the shore to help load the dead, injured and hostages into skiffs back to ships infirmaries. She says to a group of sailors coming from the beach with saltwater hoses, "Help me unfold these stretchers and pick up the wounded. Come on hurry, those hoses are the perfect protection."

Other nearby marines or buccaneers quickly offer assistance as the battle carries on. They shoot monster after monster with plenty of water-power and without hesitation.

They even blast down holes when nothing seen. Wet holes are too dangerous for the monsters to exit. Medics tape over wounds with the sulfur-enhanced salve. Some injured sailor's return to battle.

Water guns are emptying fast as full cisterns drop from three vessels for new supply. Bosons waiting on skiffs lasso them and row hard to shore as they dredge along the bottom. Dockers on shore rope them again and pull them over planks to the beach.

Wesson announces by bullhorn, "Refill skins! Beach supply, come and get it!"

Only knives and hip pistols can defend when the shooters sacks empty. Some buccaneers try unsuccessfully to poke eyes out with either blades or bullets. Demons shake blinded heads for a moment, shrug it off and come back strong. Their size and great strength overcomes many buccaneers in spite of poor eyesight. They crumble some offenders' bones and not many can get up again. The buccaneers refill and fight violently battling for victory after victory.

The lime formula treated over uniforms with rubs prevents most toxic balls from penetrating threads. Helmets luckily block headshots. Red lasers continue firing through-brown putrid air. Many demons have switched their fankdustles to fire lightning fast blue and white rays. They zigzag out tips to catch sailors without aiming. Other demons use fankdustle lasers as swords to poke sailors in the gut. More gorisilles pop up from underground.

The lead gorisille says, "Huyook, tiha glook shim fankdustle," meaning "I will crush you with my staff."

He sneaks up on a sailor, bashes the helmet, and runs. Another buccaneer looks around ready to pump down on a few demons. One sneaks up from behind catching him in a bear hug. The sailor stomps its foot and plunges a heel into its crotch. The gorisille's arms release to hold its groin. The buccaneer slips away and squirts it to death, saying, "That was for my brother. Fill a pot in hell's kitchen, you dirty devil!"

The raid progresses with great success. They have a large supply of water on the beach and it will not run out again. Larger quantities of beasts are falling and almost all of the gargies are dead. Seven-foot monsters and four-foot demonic dogs go down easier than dousing a campfire. The sailors have gained experience and are not much afraid anymore. Their fear has turned to anger. The gorisilles and gargies resort to surrounding individuals in packs. They gain advantages on sparsely infiltrated parts of the island. Many undiffused volcanos remain and Charlie is concentrating on putting them out. Some angry buccaneers seek justice with stone packed fists at gargie rock hard jaws after blasting them down. One sailor says, "How dare you look like somebody I hate," and throws a punch and after screams "Owe!"

One who watched says, "Oh that was smart are you trying to teach him how to fall down or what?"

It gives a slight satisfaction the first time. Every sailor having done so does it for the last time. It hurts. Live beasts are counting down from the thousands to the hundreds. Only 29 sailors have died and 192 wounded. Remaining gargies seek horses pulling the buckboards by command of gorisilles yelling, "Attack, attack!"

The drivers shoot them down easily before causing damage.

The few gargies left run in packs charging sailors at hatches and smother them with full body slams over mouthpieces. The others bite through uniforms while they're off guard. The sailors have killed almost all in these final attempts. Commander Wesson has his hands full with three dogs surrounding him. Ensign Fulbright saves him as his sack misfires, saying, "Oh no, you don't. Splish splash, the dogs are dead."

The commander says, "I am running out of water, buckaroos!"

He returns to the beach for a refill. Steamy, scummy fumes rise off the Lava Clan all over the island. The deluge is working in poor visibility from brownout smog. A blue sky occasionally appears as Utopio's cart pushes it back.

A gorisille leader beneath land says, "Eyat, timmons, yey nuk, cunnghing," meaning "Retreat underground!"

Nevertheless, a young trigger-happy sailor extinguishes him. One small first-class woman swabbie retrieves a fankdustle from the ground and pokes an eight-foot demon in the left eye. He catches her by the neck and lifts her up. A gargie pops up underneath her feet. She stands on its back and squirts the rounded ears off the gorisille. On her way falling to the ground, she squirts the dog to death. She again kills more popping up around.

Another sailor watching asks, "Are you alright, darlin'? You're mighty athletic but you're a darlin' anyway. Way to go!"

The brazen Lava Clan's home territory with all of its evil is about to vanish. The clan's domicile for food, drink, slop, and sleep is nearly all destroyed. Charlie rides the horse over to help sailors lift a barrel into a hatch. He pumps like a rifleman and kills five gorisilles on the way. Once there, he says, "Strong Am Himself must be saying about now, it's their end. Don't ya think? How many more can there be?

You are doing great work, men. Can I be of assistance?"

The oldest buccaneer says, "We have it sir but thanks anyway and thanks for killing them gorls. They surely were going to come after us!"

The Beaulancian navy is winning. The island is about to be put asunder. Somehow, it is as if the very island is cheering them on. The air cleanses fast as volcanos extinguish. Utopio's cart is reaching shore. Admiral Charlie, Commander Wesson and Ensign Fulbright return to the *Harmony* noticing wind over volcanos not blowing smoke toward Beautyland anymore. The sailors remove helmets and masks.

Fulbright stands next to Charlie, commenting, "The end of these volcanos will be a true relief for everyone, sir."

Charlie says, "Indeed! Peace could endure forever after this evil homeland deteriorates. The Island itself will have relief. It sheltered Lava Clan culture to its own ruin. No one will miss them."

She comments, "Some shelter, huh, sir?"

Charlie says, "The monsters lost all reason for living. This is no place to live. Wickedness is always justified through suffering. This understanding eluded them. To them a good life is bad and a bad life is good. Hot, steaming lava running through their veins and disgusting food to eat are causes for celebration in their world. Good and evil think worlds apart and finally clashed with a predetermined fate today."

"Everything good they wrongfully touched and purposely hurt," she adds.

"Whether the Lava Clan stomps on each other or foreigners, it's always about envy," Charlie opines.

A Chief Petty Officer returns from battle and overhears. He steps into the helm's deck, saying, "Yes, sir, Admiral Cavanaugh, and unfortunately they wasted our generosity long ago before the reign of Harmonious."

Charlie replies, "Aye, and it is amazing how even a beast can look a gift horse in the mouth. They extinguish easily though, don't they?"

The Commander says, "Indeed, I am amazed. If our water lands even a speck, they just melt. It seems an answer to a promise since our country turned to God. If there are other realms for eternal punishment I would hate to see where they go from here."

The Chief replies, "I think God is no longer tolerating true evil. The day is coming when all will be well with the world even here."

Charlie responds, "They acted confused in the fight, didn't they? We gave them a big surprise. I felt like an instrument of God."

The Chief remarks, "Well, sir, I tell ya, they certainly changed weapons often enough!"

Charlie answers, "They fell right into our hands as a war in futility."

The Chief comments, "They're stupid. Hate brings out the dumb in all of us."

Fulbright responds, "I second that."

Charlie reminisces, "You know how Cain the psycho hypnotized me? I could not think for myself at all. If he gets into your head, let me tell ya! He will mess you up. If we don't put an end to Evil then what do you think would happen next?"

"You mean Evil could transform everyone into monsters like the Lava Clan," asks Fulbright?

The Chief replies, "One monster stopped short of whacking my knees but went to his laser trigger instead. Was it being thoughtful? I blasted it down."

"It was not feeling sympathy, I promise! Never fall for that one Chief," says Charlie.

"I saw a human resemblance in his murderous eyes," says the Chief.

Charlie adds, "Evil was in there. He more than took advantage of their brains. You can just imagine the breeding that took place in all these years of outcast."

The Chief never saw Blaze up close, yet wants a reckoning.

Commander Wesson remarks, "The Island of Relief is safely deactivating, sir."

"The smog is greatly reducing but we need to finish all shafts before we leave," Charlie insists.

Buccaneers on the island race full buckboards across the sharp landscape. The horses pull gladly in allegiance feeling guilty for assisting demons in their cause. Each barrel explodes inside cones with the weight equivalency to hundreds of rock salt wagonloads. Layers of unbreakable and insoluble materials plaster center lava pools. The eruptions land solid coverings without a splash and cool the bubbling lava into settling.

The island quiets and sun shines through brownout for longer intervals. Utopio's cart pushes against salty ocean winds further blowing gritty clouds south into natural rainstorms miles away. It never rains on the Island of Relief. God kept it dry. Utopio hovers over the island scanning for beings.

Charlie shouts, "Don't let 'em slip away. We don't want any trouble later, go get 'em Utopio!"

Commander Wesson replies, "Few stacks remain spewing and the beasts are almost all dead. We have the upper hand, sir. The flaming stallion's roving storm dropped powder into the last live smoke stacks."

Utopio turns his head and says, "Beaulancians leave, I will finish here, return to your ships. Beautyland needs you!"

Admiral Charlie can hardly believe his ears. He looks through the spyglass, grabs a loudspeaker, and says to the whole battalion,

"Victory is ours. They have met their doom."

One sailor shouts, "Thank you magic horse, for making the devils pay! We came, we saw, we conquered."

All shout, "Hooray!"

Ship crews set booms, capstans, and straps to hoist rescued mustangs over rails into holds equipped with thirty stalls per ship.

Sailors disassembling buckboards and wagons on the shore at the four landing points skillfully install makeshift docks like an eight-slice pie. Horses have only a quarter-mile trot to safety up docks to steamers. Buccaneers leave the Island as the last twenty skiffs fill up. Surviving demons dig through flaky powder to escape the damaged underground. The heat-retarding mixture cools their internal flames and quickly kills. The entire flotilla screams joyously, and one sailor clearly shouts, "These fumes will never more erupt!"

All the hands on decks wave to Utopio, screaming, "Hooray!"

He keeps eyes over the island while parking the sky wagon directly in position to flip the whole thing over while singing,

"There is evil on the Isle of Relief. Some call them the rising runs. They ruined many a good day until now. They're done, tell your children not to do what the demons done; spend their lives in sulfuric waste on the island of the volcanic sun!"

At the perfect time, he adjusts a lever opening the cart bottom wider. He fills all holes on the island. The underground is flooded with the heat diffusing powder. Gorisilles and gargies pop up steaming like dry ice as powder avalanches suffocate them to a frigid death.

"Anchors away!" the Admiral commands.

The ships pull out with the dead and wounded accounted for. No one is missing. In looking back at the island, it resembles a powdered caramel covered series of stalagmites. It is eye candy for the Beaulancians.

Above the *Harmony*, Spirit and Astro suddenly appear in a nearly blue atmosphere performing this little ditty:

"In the sunshine where the days are stronger and the nights are longer than moon's kind. There is a free wind blowing good air. Do, do, do, do, do, do, do. The electric purple landscape has been hit by a Topio rain."

His cart is empty and the island is simmering down, any possible remaining demons and lizards will eventually solidify, they are all finished. Topio unharnesses and drops the cart upside down over the island. Its invisible walls imprison everything. He zooms away to meet Spirit and Astro and gives a wink to Charlie in passing overhead. He looks at his cousins and says, "Let's finish the fight," and all three zip off out of sight.

Charlie shouts, "Full steam ahead. Remember Relief!"

Chapter 23

THE CHASE

Jake and a handful of Indians spent the night struggling with mounted weariness in hot pursuit. Magical dust lightly illuminates landscape with translucent gold tinted swirls under footsteps in freshly returning coastal winds. Jake's pony needs rest. Blaze devised many dead-end tracks. Yesterday at a portal, Jake refilled skins, insisting Beaulancians stay inside until further notice.

"Fear not, we outnumber them," he said with confidence.

Hank and twenty Indians ride close to Jake's small band on the plateau.

"Hey, Jake, slow down. Whoa! Let me tell you, we dropped off our masks and refilled at the portal under the alligator juniper yesterday. Everyone was gone."

"Relax, Hank! Some guards went with Dulcet to defend Plentyville. Everyone else is still there deep inside the caverns. What else is going on?"

He answers, "I saw Chief Wiseoda with Takoda and warriors hunting demons in the ravine."

"I thought I was on top of Blaze several times. He lost me at each juncture. Only forty or fifty are with him. His horse has two pointed hooves. I never missed a track. Anyway, we killed most of them on the battlefield. Have you seen any running away up here?" asks Jake.

Hank explains, "No I haven't! I have seen only tracks, yours and theirs. That's all."

Jake points down beside a brave's pony saying, "Look tracks right here and a broken branch. It's them alright, pointed hoof prints, let's follow!"

"I hear riders," Hank says.

A brave in the group says, "Many warriors."

Behind sunlit aspen trees, Ben and Molly appear with several warriors guarding their flank. Molly draws in closer saying, "Good morning, anyone here hungry?"

"I am, darlin', I lost my pack of rations when Danny Boy went down," says Jake.

Molly replies, "Well, honey, you must be famished. Here, take this jerky, biscuit, and orange. Let me know if that's enough!"

Jake responds, "Thank you, but have you got enough for all of us?"

She replies, "Sure we do. Warriors pass out some vittles to these men."

They dig into packs and come out with enough food to pass around.

Jake says, "This will do just fine, let's eat!"

He bites the jerky while peeling the orange to suck juice down his dry throat. Almost a thousand warriors pull up behind Ben and Molly.

Jake shouts, "Listen up, everyone! I am following these tracks. I want Hank, Ben and two hundred warriors to come with me. The rest of you head northwest and surround Plentyville from Faith's Creek. Keep monsters inside the perimeter. Do not allow any to escape into the foothills and take no prisoners. Does anyone know where my family is?"

Molly answers, "They're with Will's several thousand warriors headed northwest. I needed more action and broke away. Several hundred warriors would not let me leave alone. We found Ben and hooked up with him."

"Well, Molly, you need to get back to Will," says Jake.

"No way, sir! Those demons tortured me on the island. I need a reckoning. I am going with you!" she exclaims.

Jake replies, "OK! You deserve a chance if you feel up to it."

Ben says to a brave behind him, "Chokwok, cut out your best warriors for us!"

"The rest of you go find Will and surround the city," Jake orders.

The Rangers choose and dress fresh horses from the warrior's remuda and cut out of there. Chokwok and a couple hundred top-notch warriors soon follow. He stops at some disturbing tracks and dismounts. Pointed marks luminously glow in the dirt.

"Hmm, hot," he says.

He remounts bareback again leading two hundred up to Jake, saying, "Chokwok track alone, warriors stay with you! I come back! Show way!"

He lunges south into a gallop toward the Blessing shifting, side to side sniffing tracks, from only two feet above the ground.

Six gorisilles pop out from behind bushes around a flagstone ledge spooking the pony. Chokwok falls off as Blaze peeks under a secret flagstone lid to caverns he used eons ago and says, "Bring him to me."

Four gorisilles grab him throwing his bow, arrows, and water skin aside. The others chase his running horse. Blaze grabs tie strings on his deerskin vest and pulls him under the lid. Scout glides helmetless in good air back from Beaver Dam noticing the struggle. The floodgates are open and fresh water is cleansing the riverbed. Two gorisilles underneath the lid open mouths shining internal flames down a flagstone staircase. Blaze pushes Chokwok rolling like a doodlebug into a wide empty chamber. He quickly stands at the bottom pointing a knife as thirty-nine gorisilles from another room enter with fankdustles. Blaze slowly follows the two light shiners downstairs under a low-brimmed hat and cape draping over steps for a grand entrance.

He asks with reptilian eyes in a deep hissing voice, "How long do you want to live, Indian? Tell me who trapped my son and I will let you go."

Chokwok spits.

Blaze fires a flaming finger torch between the Indian's legs. Chokwok closes his eyes so not caught in a trance and drops the knife saying, "Trap you too."

Blaze responds, "You tell me who or my next flame will strike."

Chokwok spits again.

Meanwhile, Scout finds Saber Toes lying in a tree on a ridge above the Blessing watching water zoom by.

He swoops down and squawking, "Get up, Saber pup."

Saber Toes responds, "Like hey, dude, life is good again."

"Not yet, my friend, Blaze in hole with Indian to defend."

Saber asks, "Dude, where's the hole, dude?"

"At the flagstone peak above the valley steep, hurry scurry, Scout worry! I go to valley below, watch Blaze to know."

He flies away as Saber jumps into motion, running over boulders and jumping from branch to branch until reaching the search party. He runs up to Jake and horses rock out-of control into frenzy. Saber races up a tree to calm everyone down. Jake orders warriors on nervous horses to scatter away in the woods.

The lion mentions, "Jake dude, Mr. Evil took an Indian into a hide-away under a flagstone cap, dude!"

"Flagstone huh, hmm, they must be at Gorgeous Flats on the rim overlooking Plenty Valley. OK, Saber, we're on our way."

A disturbance above ground distracts the Lava Clan. Warriors find Chokwok's horse. The two outside gorisilles surprise Ben and Molly grabbing their mounts bridles. The horses freak.

Jake shouts, "Stay on," and quickly douses them down.

An Indian rides over the flagstone lid saying, "Here a tussle!"

Jake dismounts, pries the lid open and orders, "Ben and Hank bring lanterns and follow me with a few braves!"

Blaze listens and nods to a gorisille as if he has them in a trap. One beast behind the Indian points a laser at the staircase and accidental-ly puts it through Chokwok's heart. He falls dead and the last breath echoes. Demons lose the element of surprise. Jake saw the flash and heard the echo. Hank passes him a lantern. He runs down the stairs with shooter pointed all the way. The Lava Clan scurries down a narrow path to the valley floor where Black Rain waits. Jake barely steps into the chamber, sees the body and shouts,

"Chokwok!"

The other Rangers rush in and the Indians right behind.

Ben says, "He's dead!"

They follow the steep path to the exit. The warriors on top place their horses with a remuda. A smell of gorisilles in the air frightens the herd. They break away in a raucous down the old lumber trail. Gorisilles emerge by the hundreds from concealing fruit trees at the bottom and trap the ponies.

Utopio intercedes whinnying from the sky and all eyes turn to him. His mane forms a massive red fire hose. The gorisilles drop to their bellies with the few remaining gargies and Utopio disappears. Wiseoda's warriors arrive over an arroyo's ridge and encircle the runaway horses. The Lava Clan plows over fruit trees in the commotion for a frantic getaway. Some warriors chase after and squirt a third of them down. The Chief looks up at the warriors on the flagstone rim pointing his bow to follow saying, "Destroy!"

Two hundred plus Indians chase down the lumber trail hooting and hollering. Their Love for the fertile valley causes sorrow in trampling over orchards. Molly hung back watching and now slowly rides down to join Takoda. The chase sends soft farmland dust blowing for miles. Flashes pop through the trees as another battle rages on. Wiseoda sees Utopio for the first time standing alone again on the rim. He glows with ears pointing to a creek. The Chief raises bow for the few remaining braves with the caught remuda to follow. They roam past the hideaway's exit to the creek.

Takoda waits on the other side saying, "Father, come see!"

He found Black Rain's pointed prints. Jake's team walking ahead on foot hears and stops. They meet and Takoda says, "Woo, ha, hook tah, ey caieyo." Meaning: "Bring their horses!"

The Rangers remount fully tacked caught horses. Takoda and Molly ride along with them to cornfields near the city. Wiseoda's unit splits off to the rolling hills through walnut orchards.

Blaze is in a cornfield, saying, "I know there is a tunnel here somewhere. I use to escape Harmonious soldiers through it eons ago. It must still be here. Help me look."

They scour the field looking for an entrance while Blaze stays mounted spotting a petrified tree stump whispering, "Here it is, I remember this," and dismounts slapping Black Rain's rump to run north.

Blaze digs away soil with long fingernails finding the long narrow tunnel and enters as a slithering serpent again but the gorisilles are too big to follow in their natural form. They blast lasers around the hole trying to make the entrance larger without success. Jake's band sees red flashes and rushes to the sight. The gorisilles point fankdustles too late. Rangers fire first, destroying all forty in less than a minute.

Chapter 24

THE DEAL

B laze is deep inside the tunnel on his way to the city. Jake dismounts and peers into the dark tunnel listening to him struggle. Warriors in orchards finish off all remaining Lava Clan there and race to corn-field action. An arriving brave speaks to Takoda saying, "No more Lava Clan. Everywhere they are dead!"

Blaze, the snake hears the comment and quiets down all alone as sneaky as possible. He considers, *"Only Black Rain remains alive,"* and looks back whispering, "I will soon control Beaulancia (bew-lan-sha) on my own. The glory is mine. Think twice you goody dumbbells; you will be my new puppets! Hiss, hiss, ha, ha!"

Wiseoda's group gallops down to the cornfields and joins the vic-tors. Utopio lifts off from the ledge in glorious splendor as a beautiful mighty steed and lands before Black Rain. He blocks the path to an open oat field and challenges him to a fight. The large mean dark horse pecks at the ground and rears.

He whinnies and says, "Ah, pelican, at last, the true you!"

His nostrils flare to shoot torching flames. Utopio stands strong against the onslaught. His lustrous coat is impenetrable.

He insists, "Stallion! I am impervious to fire. What else have you got?"

Black Rain lifts his eyelids and shoots red-hot beams at him. Still, Utopio is unscathed.

He asks, "Having fun yet?"

The taller Black Rain is furious and throws both front hooves at Utopio's head. Utopio rears and clicks hooves against hooves. Black Rain stretches to bite his neck. Utopio bobs and weaves with bites of his own and grabs hold of the dark horse's mane with his teeth. He rips a section out. Black Rain snaps at his face and nips his nose but the hide is too strong to damage. Utopio counters with a bite to the ear and hot red ooze sparkles out. Black Rain dances in circles around him, striking unsuccessfully at every turn.

Utopio catches him with a bite to the snout and again hot ooze leaks out. Black Rain turns around quickly landing a heavy power kick without any damage, not even a dimple. The mightier Utopio flexed deflecting the bam.

He remarks, "Dark stud, you are no match for me. Look into my eyes."

Black Rain faces as Utopio's eyes shoot mesmerizing yellow rays and the devilish stallion's garnet pupils change to black. He drops like a smoldering mattress.

Utopio floats up looking down and says, "I wish there was another way, Black Rain. You would have been a great horse if it were not for what Blaze made you! We could have been friends!"

Watching him die causes a slight tear. He snaps out of it zooming away to guide large mammal's home from sanctuary in the highlands. He leads from the sky with red mane flaring and tail swinging like a wand. Fall colored trees fill mountainous territory under a blue sky and sunny horizon. He directs them not to crush everything in a stampede. The Dam's released waters torrentially flush the riverbed and disperse fish again. Bobcats, raccoons, porcupines, wolves, rabbits, badgers, pine martens, and hundreds of mammal varieties return from shelters back to nature. Amphibians and reptiles return to flourish. Small creatures ride wooden rafts especially manifested and engineered by Spirit. They will not break but only glide on the mighty currents.

These four-sided straw-filled miniature arcs bring all kinds of fragile creatures safely home. Magnificent powerful radiant blue waterfalls flow from the dam. They slush smashing waves against the watercourse walls with white cleansing foams all the way down to the Peaceful Ocean. The sky and air are completely pure again. Big creatures, deer, elk, moose, bears, buffalo, mountain lions and mustangs, all happily prance home together.

Soldiers stationed at the Plenty Good Stables watch Rangers and Indians rush from the fields to the city. Jake rides out front with Wiseoda and Takoda following directly behind. The Chief stops for a moment directing many warriors to the coastal side of the city and continues with Hank, Ben and Molly, to the stables. Will Marsh, Jake's family and Thomas Cavanaugh, wait at the wagon factory for news? Indians surround the city from, Faith's Creek to the coast, in the foothills and along the rim.

The military guards every avenue in and out of Plentyville. President Dulcet recovered from his imaginary world after eating the whole cake Charlie had the servant deliver. The sugar snapped him out of it. He leads forty dragoons down Main Street on a dapple-gray gelding. It is an eerily quiet occasion aside from the flapping wings of returning pigeons, cardinals, sparrows, and barn swallows. Open doors to abandoned businesses and homes invite military investigations. Everything is intact. Remains of magic dust stir in the air as the horses walk. Loosely coated buildings unveil in light winds. Blaze is just under the Presidential Mansion about to open a spider web clogged entrance under the wooden floor.

He thinks, "*When I hid under King Harmonious's city throne, the floor was marble.*"

Dulcet reaches the end of town and says to the unit, "About face, men and ladies."

Captain Brodnick asks, "Where to now, Mr. President?"

Dulcet replies, "Well, from uptown we see Indians around the hills and downtown we see more headed for the coast, so let's go to the mansion and meet the Rangers. We may have to powwow or parlay. We should make refreshments!"

Meanwhile, Blaze reverts to the old manly physique and pulls a large platinum blade from under his cape. He cuts a four-sided breakable pattern into the floor saving the carpet and whispers, "My new digs will have no need of this. I'll have to enslave a decorator."

He pulls down the cut hatch and crawls under the carpet. The first thing he notices is the statue of Bandy and it is startles him.

He responds, "No, I didn't do it! Huh, you're not real!"

He feels the wood all around its white body and red enamel bands saying, "I'm getting out of here."

Before sneaking through the hall to the kitchen, he looks back into the office around the corner at the statue and says, "You're creepy!"

The moment he finds the stove to grab some coal for lunch the front door opens. Dulcet enters with two soldiers saying, "Martin and Lewis bring some tea to my office!"

They close the door behind. Guards at the front gate greet the Rangers. Blaze hides in the food pantry behind a curtain. The soldiers make tea with water from blasters over their shoulders.

Martin remarks, "Woo, it smells like a used bathroom in here."

Lewis replies, "Dang sure does! Grab that tray and let's get out of here!"

Blaze sneaks out after they leave the kitchen and hides under the stairs. The soldiers serve Dulcet at the office desk.

He suggests, "Sit down boys and join me. Wait where is yours? Now men get back in there and get you a cup."

They look at each other, shrug their shoulders, and Lewis responds, "Well, dang if we won't, sir."

They return to the kitchen as Blaze squeezes behind a plant in the foyer. The soldiers pour tea in the kitchen. He wanders into the office making a grand entrance with the cape and wide brimmed hat.

Unarmed Dulcet catches only a glimpse while map reading. He looks up slowly fearing who it is and then jumps abruptly to his feet.

While catching his breath, Blaze reaches hands over the desk and grabs him by the throat. His physical dominance astounds the President with fear. Blaze puts the mojo on him with red swirling eyes. Flames dance out and Dulcet pops his body backwards.

Blaze mesmerizes, "You have not seen me. I am not here. Sit down and carry on."

The President drops into the chair. Blaze shifts to the hall catching the teetotalers returning. He mesmerizes them in the same way and sets them on the sofa facing the president. He shifts again to the window at the back of the room watching soldier's line the streets. The unseen Jake, Wiseoda, Hank, Ben, and Molly converse behind trees at the gate. Takoda is at the stables arranging with four braves to go fetch Will but not the others, yet. He then gallops to The Presidential Mansion's front gate with a few remaining braves.

Jake insists, "I know we are on top of him. Will, would want to be here!"

Blaze continues watching as the Rangers passed through the gate coming closer. He can see Wiseoda's headdress and Jake's Patriot hat. He turns to the large fireplace, gets in and blends, against black walls. No one in the room says a word. Blaze listens as front guards greeting the team knock on the front door. He quietly sends ultrasonic waves to Lewis on the sofa. He gets up and answers the door. The Rangers enter as he yanks the door open and leans starry eyed against the wall.

Dulcet sits unceremoniously as Jake says, "Mr. President, can you hear me? Uh-oh Mr. President can you see me? Hey, soldier, what is wrong with him? Uh, oh, you too, Hank, where is the soldier that opened the door?"

Hank checks the foyer and the soldier is oblivious to two braves tickling his sides with arrows.

Hank shouts, "Uh-oh, Jake, the boy is dim-witted!"

Jake replies, "Blaze must be here somewhere look all around!"

The Rangers ready their squirt sacks. The office fills with people and none sees Blaze hiding in the dark fireplace.

Blaze suggests in a voice as if he is one of them, "Look!"

Everyone does and in an instant, he mesmerizes the whole group, sits them on the floor and thinks of what to do next.

He laughs, "Hahahaha," and says, "I will soon be in control again. Now, where are those stupid celestial horses?"

I remark, "Utopio, Spirit, and Astro are on the roof.

I'm right behind you Blaze! Surely, you did not mean me, did you?" He turns quickly around facing the statue with great fear, saying, "So the sculpture speaks. Bandy, it cannot be you again. No, you are not there. You are not here!"

I step out of the statue passing through it as though it were not a new dimension. I stand tall over Blaze on the carpet as a live celestial mare with beautiful might saying, "Well, Blaze Evil, what did you think? That the Almighty would allow you to escape, return, destroy, and take dominion of Beautyland. Prepare yourself king of Evil, the trial's over, I'm here to process final sentencing!"

I blow into his eyes and he falls to the ground. Utopio, Spirit and Astro enter from the fireplace in spirit form and physically stand over his dazed body. He lies on his back saying with a deeply demonic voice, "No, wait, let's make me a deal! I cannot go for splats, no, no, no can do! I cannot go for splats. They killed my son! Bring him back to life and I will stay on the island bothering no one ever again, forever! Have mercy I spared all of these people. See, everyone is still alive! I will never harm another human or anything ever again! I forgive them!"

I explain, "Cain has found the place of no return."

Utopio asks, "You forgive them? Is that a relief for you? Your Island of Relief no longer exists. Here and now Evil one, there are no other islands! "

I add, "You will join Cain instead! No need to fear water anymore, there is none there."

Blaze pleads, "How about I give you my cape and hat? Say, I am dead. I will take my ship far away and never return."

Astro replies, "Why not think of a third request if you can't get no satisfaction?"

Blaze answers, "OK! Here is the deal. Let me go!"

He engulfs in his cape and flops under Utopio's legs. He dives head first through the window to the street and casts penetrating eyes on all the soldiers outside. The celestial horses pass through walls and take to the sky, but Blaze has disappeared. Scout is on the lookout for what it is all about and sees him running. The eagle meets Utopio in midair saying, "He snuck inside the firehouse on First Street; let us go get him, we can beat, you know, I bet."

Will arrives passing broken window glass on the street and finds only empty Ranger horses at the gate? Astro points him inside the mansion. He rides through the security gate past dizzy guards to the front yard. Soldiers are snoring in slumber on the grass. He walks around the side of the Mansion to the broken window and climbs in, shouting, "Rangers, everyone, oh no, not again, Jake, Ben, Molly, wake up! Wiseoda, and Takoda, wake up! Can anyone hear me? Soldiers wake up. Indians wake up!"

I reenter the room, saying, "There is nothing you can do. Let me try."

My nostrils snort out haven's dust. Lo and behold, they all snap out of it. Jake recognizes me as the statue in full life form immediately. Utopio and Scout enter the firehouse followed by Spirit and Astro.

Scout squawks, "We know here. Smell in air."

Astro adds, "Come out, come out wherever you are!"

Spirit pretends, "Ah, he is not in here, let's try somewhere else."

Utopio plays along calling off the search. Scout flies through the pole-hole to the top floor and shouts, "Here he is. Like nobody's biz."

Blaze stands in place looking directly at Scout while leaning backwards on the kitchen counter. Scout keeps his eyes away from contact saying, "Look not at me, I will not see. My eyes closed but you be hosed!"

Blaze beams rays at him and hits the pole. Scout drops to the ground floor, saying, "We found him, studs, now mess up his duds."

Utopio breaks through the upper outside window onto the second story floor firing double eye beams. The cape deflects and in return, Blaze bombards him with torching fingers. Utopio's illustrious coat protects against the blasts. Blaze casts a useless red-hot sparking whip instead. His eyes cannot mesmerize the stallion either. He transforms into the serpent and makes a fast slither out the window. I Bandy have caught him in my teeth and throw his curling body to my back in midair.

The other two celestial studs and Scout follow me toward the sun. Way up high I rear and slide him off in a pass to Utopio. Blaze reconfigures into his Evil man's body. Utopio kicks him across the sky. He loses the hat but spreads out his cape trying to fly. Spirit catches the hairless outlaw and bucks him over to Astro who catches him in his teeth and carries him across the sky thrusting left and right, back and forth. He zooms up and down across the sky. Blaze is really shaking as Astro passes him to the back of Utopio.

He screams, "Ahhhhhh," facing the ground falling as Utopio throws him off and swoops upside down and comes under Blaze with a kick, sending him spinning past Scout. Blaze plunks face down on top of his hat on the mansions front yard in front of me.

I respond, "I have received the kick off."

Scout lands on the edge of the white mansion's roof saying,

"It is your choice to run down field or pound your hooves without yield."

Strong Am foretold to crush the head of the beast and this I choose!

Scout says to the pancake headed carcass, "Her ended ya with a real deal and given no last meal. No one will cry boo-hoo for you. I waited eons to give this speech in gratitude to no longer screech! Welcome Bandy again to the land of Beauty! I missed you since the exile, cutie! An adaptation since last we met caused my talk to rhyme, you bet. The spell is finally broken and my voice in time is now a choice for jokin'!

"Long ago Blaze cast a spell on me to kill the King. I was away flying ill through windstorms far from the spring. Bandy, you remember, I was to fetch a groundhog. Anyway, gliding over choppy waters, Blaze struck me down and paralyzed my mind. He wanted me to kill King Harmonious. The spell did not work as intended for the jerk but caused monotonous rhyming in my speech until this timing. But I am a good rhymer, am I not? Spell or no spell I am now a free bird thanks to you Folkhavenly equines!"

Utopio, Spirit and Astro meet in midair blowing rose mist through invisible trumpets and the sound travels. The victorious melody signals Charlie on the Peaceful Ocean and awakens entranced soldiers around the Mansion. The underground Beaulancians hear and exit to homes in true relief. Jake strolls over to have a closer look at the dead body. He squirts for good measure and the cape sizzles. The Rangers and family with Indians, Dulcet and soldiers put on a celebration. They dance around his carcass singing hallelujah songs fearlessly for hours giving all Beaulancians a chance to come witness.

Judy remarks, "I'm proud to be a Beaulancian and free at last. God bless Beautyland! It is amazing what faith has done.

Many people squish ceremonial streams on his smoking body, shouting, "Tis the end of Evil. Hurray!"

"Remember him not!" Scout adds.

Utopio, Spirit, and Astro watch the festivities from atop the firehouse. The grounds swirl with celestial cleansing as the party continues.

Utopio points his nose and exclaims, "Bandy is in the sky smiling and sparkling like diamonds."

Spirit adds, "Mission faithfully accomplished!"

Astro remarks, "Farewell Beautyland! Have no fear. The Blaze Evil man and Lava Clan are finished!"

Beautiful again is Beautyland inside and out! From where shall the next wickedness come and lead us to conquer? It makes no difference because our job is never done. Until a new order from central command enlists us we will eat, live and enjoy, like there is no tomorrow. We equines will forever go where trouble lurks against the good! The fight is ours. With love and duty we will perform justice on all evil to the very end. Majestic angelic horses are we four and for you we will defend. We are the horses of Folkhaven.

The fear of the lord leads to life, and he who has it will abide in satisfaction; he will not be visited with evil.
—Proverbs 19:23.

They lurk in ambush like lions in a thicket...The helpless are crushed, laid low; they fall into the power of the wicked.
—Psalms 9–10

He said, "Listen! This is what the LORD says to you: 'Do not be afraid or discouraged because of this vast army. The battle is not yours, but God's...You will not have to fight this battle. Take up your positions; stand firm and see the deliverance the LORD will give you. Do not be afraid; do not be discouraged. Go out to face them tomorrow, and the LORD will be with you.'
—2 Chronicles 20:15, 17

There is a time for everything, and a season for every activity under heaven: a time to be born and a time to die, a time to plant and a time to uproot,
a time to kill and a time to heal, a time to tear down and a time to build,
a time to weep and a time to laugh, a time to mourn and a time to dance,
a time to scatter stones and a time to gather them, a time to embrace and a time to refrain,

a time to search and a time to give up, a time to keep and a time
to throw away,

a time to tear and a time to mend, a time to be silent and a time
to speak,

a time to love and a time to hate, a time for war and a time for peace.
—Ecclesiastes 3:1–8.

ABOUT THE AUTHOR

Thomas Tyme attributes a love for horses and the amazing landscapes of the USA to this writing. He sees horses as real characters having owned and leased since 1962. Trail rides in New York, Connecticut, Montana, Colorado, Utah, Texas, Arizona, Mexico and Costa Rica, gave influence to images depicted in the story. Born in Oakland, California, into a Coast Guard family, many early on transfers brought them to New York, Connecticut, Washington, D.C., and Houston, TX...

"When someone asks where I'm from, the answer is always Texas or oh, I'm just an American," says Tyme.

He resided happily in Texas for thirty-eight years until his father's death on September 8, 2001. The funeral was September 11, 2001, and the incident led to the formation of this story. Tyme's love for Christianity gives way in "Protecting Beauty" to the strange and mystical resourcefulness heavenly horses must possess. He says,

"They can move mountains!"

Thomas Tyme wearing a handmade Tom Folkhaven© Patriot hat
as mentioned in the story.

33900747R00122

Made in the USA
Columbia, SC
11 November 2018